HOME REMEDIES

STORIES

XUAN JULIANA WANG

HOGARTH

London / New York

Copyright © 2019 by Xuan Wang Inc.

All rights reserved.
Published in the United States by Hogarth, an imprint of the Crown Publishing Group, a division of Penguin Random House LLC, New York.
crownpublishing.com

HOGARTH is a trademark of the Random House Group Limited, and the H colophon is a trademark of Penguin Random House LLC.

The following stories have been previously published: "For Our Children and For Ourselves" in *The Atlantic,* "Home Remedies for Non–Life-Threatening Ailments" in *The Brooklyn Rail,* "White Tiger of the West" as "Grandmaster Wu Eats Glass" in *Day One,* "FuErdAi to the Max" in *Narrative,* "Days of Being Mild" and "Algorithmic Problem Solving for Father-Daughter Relationships" in *Ploughshares.*

Library of Congress Cataloging-in-Publication Data
Names: Wang, Xuan Juliana, 1985– author.
Title: Home remedies : stories / Xuan Juliana Wang.
Description: First edition. | London ; New York : Hogarth, [2019]
Identifiers: LCCN 2018038559 | ISBN 9781984822741 (hardback) |
ISBN 9781984822758 (trade paperback) | ISBN 9781984822765 (Ebook)
Subjects: LCSH: Chinese Americans—Fiction. | BISAC: FICTION /
Literary. | FICTION / Short Stories (single author). | FICTION /
Cultural Heritage.
Classification: LCC PS3623.A4587 A6 2019 | DDC 813/.6—dc23 LC record
available at https://lccn.loc.gov/2018038559

ISBN 978-1-9848-2274-1
Ebook ISBN 978-1-9848-2276-5

Printed in the United States of America

Jacket design by Elena Giavaldi
Jacket photograph by No.223

10 9 8 7 6 5 4 3 2 1

First Edition

To Mom and Dad, for letting me chase my dreams

献给,让我追逐梦想的爸爸妈妈

CONTENTS

HOME REMEDIES

FAMILY

Mott Street in July

ABOVE THEIR SLEEPING heads hung the wedding photo. It had hung there before any of the children were even born. Walnut, Pinetree, and Lucy would sleep in a row, pressed up against Mama's soft warmth. The spot on the bed closest to the door was left empty, so that whenever he got home the children wouldn't stir. That was their baba, of course.

There they were, Mama and Baba, a part of history. It was still the good part. Mama in a red dress, her hair shiny and voluminous, her lips the color of jewels. With a curl above his brow and the wedding studio's white suit on, that was the happiest Baba had ever looked. He never smiled like that in real life.

The family lived in a one-bedroom apartment on the second floor of 24 Mott Street. Mama and Baba with two boys and a baby girl, who started out as toddlers at the Catholic preschool on Mosco Street. As they grew taller, they walked past the screaming babies on their way to elementary school and looked down their noses at those maniacs. Each morning they stood beside the deep kitchen sink that they had once bathed in, tickling one another with their elbows and squishing toothpaste foam between their toes. If the telephone on top of the fridge rang, the tangled cord stretched over their wet heads and together they screamed with delight at the thought of being electrocuted.

Each afternoon Walnut, Pinetree, and Lucy walked the path through Roosevelt Park, leaning on the partition to watch the kites go up over the shrubs on Forsyth. It did not yet boggle their minds that the insides of those things that fly also look like the insides of those that swim. They had yet to question why the bones of a fish could look like the bones of a kite. They had not known to wonder how far to look back in history for the connection. Instead, the three children raced up the stairs to the window to count the black cars that lined Mosco Street for funerals four times a week, because Pinetree said that the more black cars there were, the more that dead person was loved.

These streets held their first universe. Under this patch of sky, where melting ice slid over the sidewalks and cars competed for space with supermarket carts teetering with recycling, that was all there was.

It went on this way for a long time, until the children got their first bunk beds and their world stretched upward to the brass ceiling tiles. When he turned thirteen, Walnut wordlessly installed a curtain across the room with his disproportionately large hands. From then on, the children no longer saw Mama and Baba before they drifted off to sleep.

But in the years when all five slept on the same pieced-together bed, in the same room, Lucy would often wake in the dark to see Baba climbing under the covers beside Mama, and she guessed that that was the reason why it was she and not her brothers who felt closest to him.

As their bodies grew larger, the empty space around them grew thick and heavy with riches they brought inside to make theirs. Blue jeans, comic books, two computers, and a stuffed dog that told jokes. Walnut helped Baba make room for a wardrobe that would partly block the doorway to the bedroom, so that they had to turn sideways in order to walk through. There was nowhere for clothes to disappear to, except for when they were drying, which was done either out on the fire escape or up on the black tar roof. Old bricks held on to the nails that carried their washcloths, flyswatters, and supermarket calendars, as well as the antenna that allowed the television to see all the way to China.

The front door began to stay open, to let fresh air flow through the hallways, past the neon-colored bins where they kept their meager treasures, day after day, until the plastic lost its brightness.

Soon there wasn't enough room for all of them inside, and Lucy took her time studying the tiny cardboard iPhones and sports cars in the funeral parlor's windows, before she walked past Mama, who played poker with the other ladies on the corner of Mulberry and Bayard, under the lights of the twenty-four-hour parking lot. Whenever one of them entered the apartment, they avoided the others' eyes as a courtesy. Walnut was always chatting on his laptop, and even though he would have liked to be outside, Pinetree didn't have a fixie bike or a skateboard, so eventually he had to do what Walnut did and play on another laptop. Then Walnut got glasses, Pinetree broke his wrist, Lucy needed braces, and Baba had to take a second job at a mechanics shop deep enough into Brooklyn that they never saw him.

That was the year they started calling him "Dad."

Dad lifted weights at the YMCA, wore a thick gold chain around his neck, and started drinking beer in big glass bottles instead of in cans. He stopped sitting down to the broths and steamed fish that Mom cooked on the stove and would instead lie on the bottom bunk in front of the television with a white Styrofoam container of BBQ duck rice balanced on his chest.

He ate quickly, his hands blackened from soot, not speaking to them even if they asked him a question. He snapped at them for any reason, as if they were somehow mysteriously to blame for his aching back. Lucy's brothers didn't know how to receive Dad's affections, so they stopped trying to earn them. But while Walnut faced his computer in silence and Pinetree flipped through basketball comics, Lucy studied Dad until he told her to stop. His arms had gotten more tanned and even more muscular. If she and her brothers were changing with each passing day, then her parents must be as well, and even if no one would tell her why, she wanted to know how. She alone searched for the opening into the concealed passageways that wound through each of her parents' hearts, into the things they didn't tell her about.

After all, it was Lucy who noticed the tattoo of a black and red carp that had grown across Dad's lower belly, the flickering fish tail peeking out from beneath the hem of his white shirt. Lucy imagined the carp swimming across her father's belly when he turned in his sleep, moving up to his chest to feed on his snores. Maybe the red scales leaped out when Dad was feeling brave and dove deep into his heart if he was ever afraid.

The fish was born on Dad's belly in May. Then it became June, and all reports forecasted the hottest summer on record. One humid day led to another, then another. Before the televised fireworks on the Fourth of July, the Asian carp crisis was announced by the U.S. Fish and Wildlife Service. On the news, reporters on the scene described the carp as roughly the size of dolphins and some that had grown to be the size of economy sedans.

"Like pigs, the Asian carp root around in the dirt for food," said a Michigan senator to the press. "It's not just that they're muddying our scenic lakes, but they're damaging the integrity of the bio composition of American waters by causing loss of vegetation and agricultural runoff."

Discomforting close-ups of the carps' giant mouths swallowing air above the water played on a loop. Since Asian carp had no natural predators, the reporters went on to explain, they ate all the other fish, as well as the turtles on the bank. . . . They ate the frogs and the birds, too, if they got close enough to the water. . . . And they ate a few adorable dogs right off a dock!

Destroyed leisure boats.

Killed *heritage* waterfowl.

Leaped onto the decks of ferries and *terrorized* innocent passengers.

When pressed to share the committee's possible solutions, the director of the U.S. Fish and Wildlife Service said with a sad shake of his head, "I wish I could ask our Americans to eat our way out of this mess, but who's going to want to eat such bony fish! I mean how much gefilte fish can one nation really make?"

The most charismatic spokesperson of the anti-fish movement was a retired Great Lakes police officer. "I've tried trapping them, seining, poisoning them, but even the dead *[bleep]* carp are stinking our docks. I just can't *[bleep]* wait to get rid of them, and they must be gotten rid of. They are to blame for every *[bleep bleep bleep bleep bleep]*! If they destroy the commercial fishing of our Great Lakes, what will we *[bleep]* do?"

The fortune-telling grandmothers on Bayard and Mulberry, who began conversing regularly with a spiritual grandmaster via WeChat, were the first to recognize the urgency. Lucy watched as they dusted the sunflower shells off their puffy vests, stretched their aching joints, and hung a red banner across the benches that lined Columbus Park's crooked pathways. Wobbling on their folding stools, they ordered the bands of singers to give them their portable microphones and shut up and listen.

"The Asian carp crisis has appeared in our time to give our people a purpose, you see," they cried with their toothless mouths, "and the purpose is a worthy one."

The oracle with the bent back doubled her efforts at tossing gold-plated joss paper into her burning bucket, which was stationed right in front of a Citi Bike station. Like ghostly butterflies, the paper transformed into ancestral smoke, which floated through the park, reaching the barefoot old men who sang while their wives gyrated to communal aerobics. Her smoke carried a message and the message reached the boys on the basketball court, who sweated out things they did not understand, and even caught up to the deliverymen on their electric scooters, who were riding by as if they were being chased.

"You are the Fish Generation," the oracle grandmother whispered into the paper before dropping it into the fire. At least that's what it said on the banner to those who could read it.

Lucy watched as word spread mouth-to-mouth through the networks of public parks, Ping-Pong associations, karaoke clubs, and gambling leagues. The Asian carp could be lured with moon cakes and rice noodles to swim alongside chartered boats across the ocean, back to the waters where the carp belonged, but it was up to the Fish Generation to guide them back to their rightful home.

Though her brothers couldn't be bothered to keep up with neighborhood folklore, they couldn't argue with the fact that, in the days that followed, dishes no longer came out nearly as quickly from take-out windows, and soup dumplings often broke apart before they even got into people's mouths. Socks were being mismatched at the WashNFold and, for the first time in anyone's memory, Chinese food delivery was just as slow as any other food delivery.

The oracles said that precisely around the time Chinatown's ancestors sailed from the southern villages of Kaiping to California to work on the railroads, Asian carp were being introduced to American waters. Inspired by the sophistication of Austrian royalty, the princes of the new world imported the prized carp to breed in this vast, previously carp-free land. The bred carp were supposed to clean up the overdeveloping plankton that were turning rivers green.

Like other immigrants to the United States, each new generation of carp grew to be larger than the previous one. The carp lived and spawned in waters where native fish could not, and would not, live. Since they were entirely dependent on natural food, the carp worked hard to survive. They overcame drained rivers, years of drought, and they conquered the hazards of human and industrial waste. Floods pushed them from rivers into lakes. They moved through the country's most polluted waters, always striving, improving themselves, and trying their best to live to the fullest extent of their lifespans.

During the second week of July, Dad walked out the door of 24 Mott Street with a duffel bag of clothes and never came back. Walnut was sixteen, Pinetree fifteen, and Lucy had just turned twelve. Still, none of them followed to find out where he was going. They couldn't see what road he took to greater desires, and they didn't know where those roads would lead them.

Mom called the police. "Can you believe it? He said he never loved me." She made Walnut translate it to the blank-faced officer at the door. "Not ever. He always loved holding that over me."

Lucy thought Mom would be happy that Dad was gone. Hadn't she always complained that she was like a fire he kept putting out little by little? Shouldn't she be glad there was nobody left in the apartment who would be upset at her for drinking all the bottles of Hennessy in the glass-fronted cabinet and filling them back up with oolong tea? If she wanted to get into another fight with the shopkeeper downstairs and threaten to chop him up with a cleaver, Dad wouldn't be there to shush her and drag her home by the hair.

Yet that night Mom cried for the first time that any of them could remember. She chose to frame the story like this: Mom and Dad had a marriage of love. It was not entirely accurate to say that they enjoyed each other's company; she never had an opinion he did not disagree with and no slight was small enough for him to simply brush off. Theirs was a Chinese love. It was not about making each other happy. It was about sacrifice. It was a love devoted to suffering for the beloved. They were supposed to sacrifice over and over again for each other, each getting a turn to give up something he or she did not want for the other, until one of them died.

Lucy always thought of her mom as someone under the sea. She used to tell her friends that her mom was a mermaid, which was the brilliant excuse for why they never got to see her. Whenever she was at home, Mom was on the new cordless phone in the kitchen, speaking in a dialect they couldn't understand. She was the only one who ever broke the household rule of considerate silence.

She complained that her children took their lives for granted and that she embarrassed them, and they, in turn, resented her. Even though they saved up to buy her a leather purse last Christmas, she continued to carry the fake designer one she had bought herself from a hawker on Canal Street.

Lucy appreciated her. She really did. Yet she just couldn't say that she loved her. Tell her that she was grateful and that she was sorry for the way things turned out. There was too much between them for that. There was no happiness without sorrow, no love without pity. While the cop finished his report, the youngest child touched the top of her mom's head, and she hated her. And she loved her. She hated her and she loved her.

What made Lucy feel guilty was that part of her wished that Mom would die. Mom was just so unhappy; Lucy couldn't understand how it could possibly be worth it to live like that. She was fat as a seal. What fairness was there that Dad got to stay this great sculptural masterpiece and Mom was like some kind of leftover piece of dumpling dough? It was obvious that Dad didn't love her at that moment, but why did she have to go that far, to say that she was never lovable?

Lucy didn't know how to help her, so she thought the best possible solution would probably be for her mom to be dead.

But Mom survived. Even as the furniture, appliances, and people in the apartment fell apart around her.

A week later, caravans of roaches ran for cover each time Lucy opened the sticky kitchen cabinets. Holes appeared in the neckbands of their T-shirts. The water in the toilet ran day and night, the lever held together by two safety pins and a paperclip. Pinetree stopped going to school and not one person tried to talk him out of it. One morning the big window popped out of its frame and smacked Walnut right on the head.

"It's okay I guess," he said, in the voice he used when he was lying. "I didn't feel it in my spine or anything."

They lost the dining room table under piles of clothes, so for dinner they held their bowls on top of the newspaper spread over the lower bunk bed, picking at warmed-up take-out food sliding back and forth on a plastic plate.

"I used to be beautiful," Mom told them one night. "You don't even know! All you see is this ugliness. I don't blame you. I never finished school. I don't know anything. I feel bad that I couldn't show you anything else."

They half expected Mom to say something delusional like, "When your dad comes back, we'll be one big happy family." But, to their relief, Mom just sat at home, lifting her foot up if any of them had to walk past her, staring at them without even raising one of her going-blue tattooed eyebrows.

Then one morning Mom put on makeup, crossed the intersection at Bowery and Division, and took the bus to Atlantic City to gamble at the Tropicana casino.

That night she came home with a different hair color and a completely new set of clothes, drifting through their front door on a cloud of stale cigarette smoke with her winnings in one hand and a casino burrito in the other.

Lucy watched her, mouth opened by the front teeth she'd yet to grow into, as Mom jumped on the bed without taking off her shoes.

Mom said that an oracle grandmother on the bus told her that the tide in her fortune had changed and now she was lucky. Her good mood was a relief to all of the children, even if it made them realize that their mom didn't belong to them, not entirely.

. . .

It got so hot that summer someone mercifully broke open the fire hydrant in front of their window on Mott Street. Water drenched the neighborhood until shivering children ran home to sleep, as the asphalt washed itself into the drain. The water hitting the sheet-metal roof of the makeshift store below didn't wake them, nor did they stir with the passing of garbage trucks at dawn. In her sleep, Lucy heard nothing but the rhythm of her brothers' breaths, their comfortable shifting bodies. She must have imagined her mother kissing them on their foreheads before leaving because somehow she already knew it would happen. Just the way Mom always threatened she would. She thought they all did.

What day of the week was it? Lucy didn't know. Had she kept track, it would have made her complicit. After washing the sleep from her eyes, she noticed some bath towels were missing. A few photographs were gone, too, along with her mom's passport. She woke up her brothers and the three of them collectively decided to lie back down to take in this information: Walnut on the top bunk staring at the ceiling; Lucy staring at the wall, Pinetree staring at the back of Lucy's head, and pigeons cooing behind the walls. Their own secret birds cooed inside each of their chests.

"Isn't it obvious?" said Lucy. "First they get the fish tattoo, then they joined the Fish Generation."

Her brothers did nothing to encourage her to continue. Walnut threw a sock at the ceiling and caught it with his knees.

"After Baba got the tattoo, they packed up their things, stifling their feelings, and left in secret without any promises to return," she said. "That's the Fish Generation. That's just what they do."

Lucy chose to frame the story like this:

Mama followed Baba, who followed his heart.

Fish followed the river, the father followed the fish, the mother followed the father, and the children, holding their arms out, did not have a past to chase. Love could be a burden, too. That night, in the room Lucy had slept in all her life, she wondered if their father would be sad to have to kill the fish. If their mother would be motion sick. What must it feel like, being on those waves repeating themselves across all the oceans, pulling away and then coming back again, spilling forward up to the edge of the horizon?

The fish themselves must be confused, too. The carp hadn't done anything wrong. They weren't even genetically modified. They lived for more than a hundred years in these American waters and felt a lot of anguish and confusion, which they passed down to their own fish children. Being brought here and then raised to feed a burgeoning population, they thought they were performing a noble duty. They had a purpose. It was not their fault they adapted so well. Their fish souls must be aching with unanswered questions. They had come so far and done what was asked of them; now they were unwanted.

Sometime later the three of them sat down by the window ledge and watched a funeral procession pass by on Mott Street, but if Lucy blinked, she could see that morning's new bride stepping out of a limo in front of the Church of the Transfiguration. If she blinked again, she could see the big black hearse rolling past.

On the apartment walls, underneath the white paint thick as fabric, was blue paint, green paint, and white paint again. The fluorescent bulbs that came in coils went from yellow to orange, then flickered out, and new ones were purchased at the hardware store. Dusty, tangled plastic blinds got replaced with supermarket calendars. The smell of herbal soup, rich with long-boiling ginger root, grabbed ahold of the clothes that would become too small for them and have to be given away.

They would have liked to ask Mom and Dad what they thought they'd lost out on by living as a family all these years, but Lucy knew she wouldn't be able to. What if they knew exactly? What if they didn't?

A handful of days remained in August, and after those were over, it would still be summer.

Scribbled postings appeared on the doors of restaurants, looking for new noodle pullers and deliverymen, and those jobs were quietly filled. Nobody was expecting the children and they had nowhere to go. They were still small and stooped and unacquainted with rooms big enough to fit them. It would take more time to figure out what all this new freedom meant.

Lucy believed what the oracle grandmothers said: There was a saying, centuries old, that every thirty years, fortunes changed completely. If you looked hard enough you might find specific instances that proved it in the personal history of every family. Paid-off properties suddenly got confiscated and the owners were tried for corruption. A good son built a soy-sauce business, but then his own son was kidnapped and returned without earlobes. An old man buried all his gold in his backyard, only to forget exactly where. Ugly children grew to be as handsome as movie stars. Their children's children married charismatic artists and acquired their debts. Naughty boys yelled next to their grandfather's hospital bed, his conscious mind rocking around his unconscious body that couldn't block out the question, "Where did you bury all *our* money?"

The siblings knew about secrets. They were familiar with truths no one else believed in. Living in such close proximity, they knew there were real reasons and fake reasons and double reasons for everything. Where the official temple was and what building the unofficial one currently occupied. The real bank that looked like a fake bank and the fake bank that was actually a fake bank. Where the gang members hung out and where they pretended to hang out. The siblings knew that they had a story worth believing, something they could hold on to in case they needed it, until they didn't.

Lucy thought that meant somewhere in the world there was a Samoyed that was irritably hot, its entire life spent in Arizona, but his puppy's puppies ran free in snowy pastures on a ski resort. Then it was possible that Walnut would one day move to Brooklyn and meet the white girl of his dreams, and Pinetree would wake up in a dorm room so big he wouldn't be able to believe it, and she could sublet their apartment to an overzealous hipster couple. But how was she supposed to calculate which generation she and her brothers belonged to? Which generation did their mom and dad? Where were the three of them in the process? How would anyone know when to start counting?

. . .

In a future July, Lucy's twin boys would learn to read, at the same moment her parents' eyes would no longer see. Just when her sons learned to like the taste of bitter melon, her own parents would forget how to swallow. In time it became clear to Lucy that there were some things about love she could grasp, but that other things might be forever out of her reach.

Rumors continued to reach the siblings that the mass relocation of a problematic fish population, so cleverly devised by retired sailors, had mobilized a nationwide community of immigrants. Lucy was shocked that the citizens of Chinatown carried on as they always had. They grumbled about their commute; they socialized their dogs; they waited in line for fresh tofu.

Walnut found an article about it on *Grub Street*. From uncredited sources, it said that the main methods were spearing and shooting—with only a small mention of netting. Sure, the carp were just "beyond natural biomass," but that just meant they were "well fed" and the very definition of organic and thereby perfectly edible. Someone in the comment section wrote, "Those Chinese, they will eat anything, apparently."

Around this time, an Australian backpacker disappeared on a trip to the Three Tigers Gorge, an airplane carrying two hundred people disappeared from radar, and the media began reporting on pregnant women appearing by the dozen on the suburban streets of Los Angeles. The news channels showed ladies walking in rows under brightly colored umbrellas when there was not a cloud in the sky.

One day the fire hydrant got turned off and men in hard hats brought a cement truck and the road was fixed. A breeze carried with it the first chill of autumn. Squirrels chased each other up trees. School would start again in the fall and concerned adults, without the benefit of luck or magic, would eventually get involved in their lives. But before that had to happen, Walnut, Pinetree, and Lucy saw their parents one more time.

They were on their way to Rockaway Beach. As the express train rushed through the tunnel, the local train going in the same direction pulled up alongside. In those moments, the two trains were racing side by side. Lucy was the first to spot them and she grabbed her brothers; they pressed their faces against the glass.

Mama and Baba.

For a moment they looked exactly as they had in their wedding photo. Lit up with life and color. For just those few seconds, the five of them were together in motion, so close. Then the two cars diverged onto different paths, the parallel car became just a memory, and the children saw the water, the bridge, and the sun.

Days of Being Mild

IT TAKES REAL skill to speed down the packed streets of the Zhongguancun district of Beijing, but the singer with the mohawk is handling it like a pro. His asymmetrical spikes are poking the roof of his dad's sedan, so he's compensating by tilting his head slightly to the left.

We are meeting with a new band to talk about shooting their music video. Sara is here to deal with the script details and she is leaning all the way forward to talk concept with the two guys up front. Sara's long platinum blond hair is wavy and tumbling down her skinny back and Benji's got his fingers in her curls. His other arm is pinching a cigarette out the window.

I'm staring at the women rhythmically patting their babies while selling counterfeit receipts and listening to taxi drivers ask about one another's families as their cars slide back and forth.

Teenage part-timers are throwing advertisements in the air like confetti and somehow we're managing not to kill anyone.

The band's name is Brass Donkey and they're blasting their music from the tiny speakers of the sedan. They sound a lot like Jump In on Box, the all-girl orbit-pop band that just got signed to Modern Sky Records. I'm digging the sound, but nobody asks for my opinion.

We finally make our way to the singer Dao's apartment and more band members show up. He sits us down on the couch, and even though it's only noon, he offers us Jack Daniel's and Lucky Strikes. There are piles of discs everywhere and stacks of DVD players that the bootleg DVDs keep breaking.

"So this video, we want it to really stand out. We're really into Talking Heads right now, you know them? Talking Heads?"

The drummer turns on the TV and David Byrne appears, jerking his head back and forth to his own beat. All the band members are talking to us at once.

"We're no-wave Funstrumental, but we sound Brit pop."

"For this video we want something perversely sexual, like really obscene."

They look expectantly at Benji and Sara.

"Yeah, like really fucking sick, you know?"

"The more perverted the better!"

"Then we want this video to be blasting in the background during our debut performance at the next Strawberry Festival, on the big monitors."

I smoke their cigarettes. "Aren't you afraid of the police coming in and shutting it down?"

"That would be spec-fucking-tacular! It would be great to be shut down, even better if you could get us banned. Actually, let's make that a goal," says the singer, sinking back into his chair and turning up the music.

I watch Sara look down at her notes and then look up at me. I shrug. Benji stands up to leave and shakes everybody's hand. Then we're out of there. I can't wait to tell JJ and Gangzi, they'd definitely get a kick out of this story.

As for the video, we'll do it if we feel like it, see how it goes.

We are what the people called *Bei Piao*—a term coined to describe the twentysomethings who drift aimlessly to the northern capital, a phenomenal tumble of new faces to Beijing. We are the generation who awoke to consciousness listening to rock and roll and who fed ourselves milk, McDonald's, and box sets of *Friends*. We are not our parents, with their loveless marriages and party-assigned jobs, and we are out to prove it.

We come with uncertain dreams but our goal is to burn white-hot, to prove that the Chinese, too, can be decadent and reckless. We are not good at math or saving money but we are very good at being young. We are modern-day May Fourth–era superstars, only now we have MacBooks. We've read Kerouac in translation. We are marginally employed and falling behind on our filial-piety payments, but we are cool. Who is going to tell us otherwise?

Five of us live in part of a reconverted pencil factory outside of the fourth ring, smack in the middle of the 798 art district. We call our place The Fishtank and it covers four hundred square meters of brick and semi-exposed wall insulation. Before it became our home, it used to function as the women's showers for the factory workers. As a result, it is cheap and it is damp. The real Beijing, with its post-Olympic skyscrapers, stadiums, and miles of shopping malls, rests comfortably in the distance, where we can glance fondly at the glow of lights while eating lamb sticks.

Our roommates include JJ, the tall, dark-skinned half-Nigerian from Guangzhou, who is loudmouthed and full of swagger. He keeps his head shaved, favors monochromatic denim ensembles, and is either drinking or playing with his own band Frisky Me Tender. The resident cinematographer is Benji, who is so handsome waitresses burst into fits of giggles when taking his orders. He is working on a series about migrant workers whom he dresses in designer labels. Benji, whose Chinese name we've forgotten, was renamed by his white girlfriend, Sara, a former research scholar who has since found it impossible to leave. Sara, with her green eyes and blond hair, speaks with an authentic marbled northeastern Chinese accent, and somewhere along the line she became one of us as well. There is Gangzi from Wenzhou, the photographer who shoots product photos of new consumer electronics as well as an ever-rotating roster of models from Russia and Hong Kong. Some of them keep us company when they are sufficiently drunk. Then there's me and I'm short like Gangzi, but sometimes I can't help but feel like someone accidentally photoshopped me into this picture.

I'm a so-called producer and what that really means is that I just have more money than the rest of them. Actually my dad does. My family's from Chong Qing, where my dad made a fortune in real estate and has more money than he can spend. After I dropped out of the Beijing Film Academy, I've been hiding from my dad for more than a year and living off the money I got from selling the BMW he gave me. I said I'd try to make it as a filmmaker, but I'm low on talent. Lately, I've been watching a lot of porn.

Our apartment is just around the corner from our new favorite bar See If, and that's where Benji, Sara, and I go after our meeting. See If is three stories of homemade wood furniture and plexiglass floors. The drinks are named If Only, If Part, If Together, If No If, and so on. The alcohol is supposed to supplement your mood, but it basically all tastes the same. JJ and Gangzi and a bunch of part-time male models are all there jamming together. JJ is walking around suggestively strumming everyone's guitar.

Benji says to the group, "Hey, you have to hear the story about our meeting with the Brass Donkey guys. I think they want to get publicly flogged."

I get passed a pipe and smoke something that makes me feel like I'm vaguely in trouble. I concentrate on looking at my friends and feel swell again.

JJ cuts in. "Dude, today a cabdriver point-blank asked me how big my dick was." We listen to that story instead. Being a half-black Chinese guy, JJ is used to attention.

With the 2008 Olympics finally behind us, Beijing is getting its loud, openmouthed, wisecracking character back. The cops stopped checking identity papers on the street and all of us *Bei Piao* are letting out a collective sigh of relief as life goes back to normal.

But then this thing happened. Last week I received an email from my father. He was going to give me, his only son, the opportunity to make my own fortune. He purchased a dozen oil rigs in Louisiana and is getting the L-1 investment visa ready for me to move there and manage them. It has been decreed that my piece-of-shit ass is going to move to the United States and make use of itself. In his mind, what was I doing drifting around in Beijing with hipsters when there's an oil field in Louisiana with my name on it?

In the spring, we test-shoot the music video on our roof and even though it's a Wednesday, I make a few calls to modeling agencies and within the hour half a dozen models are strutting across our tiles wearing nipple pasties and fishnets. Sara's the one posing them in obscene variations, asking them to take their clothes off. She can get away with almost anything because she's a white girl who speaks Chinese and everybody likes her. Benji's doing the actual filming while Gangzi takes stills. Sometimes I load some film, but mostly I just drink beer and enjoy the atmosphere.

Just as the sun is whimpering its way down the side of the sky, the last girl shows up. She is a model from Hong Kong who renamed herself Zi Yang, The Light. She's got a good face, but like most girls who assume they deserve nice things, she is extremely unfriendly. Then, just as everyone is packing up to go, she emerges naked from the apartment wrapped in Gangzi's blue bedsheet. Her waist-length black hair licks at her face, her arms gather the bouquet of fabric against her small breasts, and the sheet clings to the silhouette of her long legs. Sitting among our coffee cups and cigarettes, the rest of us hardly notice her; we smile at her but not much more.

Not Gangzi.

He ties his hair into a ponytail, picks up his medium format lens, and follows her onto the tile roof like a puppy. He takes her hand and helps ease her bare feet onto the chimney.

With the sheet dripping around her, she looks ten feet tall and glorious. She lowers the sheet and ties it around her waist, covers herself with her hair, and looks away, purring like a cat, in a halfhearted bargain for attention.

So there's Gangzi, from whose lips escapes a "My God," and he fumbles with filters and straps to get the perfect photo of her. The loose tiles creak beneath his feet.

"You're gorgeous, too gorgeous," he said. "You should father my children or marry me, whatever comes first."

Sara whispers to me, "I think this is going to be trouble." And I know just as well as everyone else that Gangzi's falling for this girl and it isn't going to be pretty.

If we could grant Gangzi one wish, he'd probably wish to marry a tall girl. A very tall, very hot girl. He claims that he wants to give his children a fighting chance. Can we really blame him though? Even if he only claimed to be of average size for a man, he's probably only five three—in the morning, after he's taken a big breath and holds it. Most of the time the poor guy has to buy shoes in the children's department.

But all that is bullshit, it's just for show. Gangzi, perpetually heartbroken Gangzi, is the only one of us who can still memorize Tang Dynasty poetry, is always the first to notice if sorrow crosses any of our faces. I guess deep down we could all see that his wants were so simple—to be loved, respected, and not tossed away, for his meager holdings on this earth. It was all the wrong in him that made him so special and we were all protective of him, ready to hurt for him like we would hurt for no one else.

After the shoot is over, we go across town to D-22 to hear JJ's band perform. D-22 is the first underground punk rock club literally screamed into existence by foreign exchange students in the university district. JJ is opening for Car Sick Cars whose hit song is five-minute repetitive screaming of the words "Zhong Nan Hai," which is both the Beijing capitol building and the most popular brand of cigarettes among locals. Foreigners love it, and the audience throws cigarettes on the stage like projectile missiles.

When JJ and his band hit the stage, it's obvious that he's wasted and he tips over the mike stand as he gyrates in his Adidas tracksuit. He is singing in English, "I trim girls all night long, white and black, I know how to trim those." It's Cantonese slang for "hit on girls," coarsely translated into English, being yelled through a broken mike. These lyrics are new, probably bits of conversation he'd heard earlier that day, grammatically Chinese with clauses that don't finish, lyrics that don't make sense. We all know he kind of sucks, but so does everybody else and everyone's liking it. The Chinese groupies who took day-long buses into the city just to see the show are thrashing their heads from side to side as if they're saying "No no no" when they're really saying "Yes yes yes." JJ finishes the set by jumping off the stage and feeling up a drunken Norwegian girl who doesn't seem to mind.

Like everyone else I know, JJ drinks a ton. Unlike everyone else, he doesn't seem to want to make it big. He says he just doesn't see the use of being a hardworking citizen. I can't argue with that. I know most ordinary people will work their whole lives at some stable job and yet they'll never be able to afford so much as a one-bedroom in Beijing proper.

When the next band starts plugging in their instruments, Sara goes to mingle with the Canadian bar owner while JJ joins Benji and me by the bar.

"I am not writing for record labels. I just want to write music for the humiliated loser, the guy that gets hassled by the police, the night owl with no money who loves to get drunk," he says. I don't know if he knows that his description doesn't include someone like me, but we toast to it anyway.

We all go clubbing in Sanlitun at a place called Fiona. A once-famous French architect purportedly designed it in one hour. Every piece of furniture is a unique creation, and as a result, it looks like a Liberace-themed junkyard. Rainbow, an old acquaintance who runs a foreign modeling agency, is throwing a birthday party for herself.

"Can you believe I'm turning twenty-nine again?" she says as a greeting while she ushers us into her private room. She kisses everyone on the mouth and presses tiny pills into our hands.

"Oh, to be young and charming, I can't think of anything more fabulous," she says in her signature mixture of Chinese and English as she drapes her arms around a new model boy-friend. His name is Kenny or Benny, and he looks like a skinny Hugh Jackman. He is obviously a homosexual, but that's just not something Rainbow has to accept.

The DJ spins funky house tracks and the springboard dance floor floods with sweaty people who pant and paw at each other. Old businessmen drool at foreign girlfriends who lift up their skirts on elevated cages. Rainbow buys the drinks and toasts herself into oblivion, grooving around the dance floor yelling at the foreigners to "go nuts to apeshit!"

I can't find Gangzi or Benji, so instead I try striking up a conversation with the skinny Hugh Jackman. He asks me to teach him Chinese so I start by pointing to the items on the table.

"This is a bowl," I say.

"Bowa! Ah bowl!" he says with a shit-eating grin on his face.

"Shot glass." I push it across the table toward him.

"Shout place," he slurs, laughing. "Oh yeaah, shout place!"

It's a good thing he's handsome, I think. I want to leave, but I'm too high to wander around looking for my friends. I stick by the bar for a bit and talk to the attractive waitresses who swear they've met me before, in another city, in another life, and I am sad that they have nothing to say to me but lies.

Beijing is a city that is alive and growing. At any given mo-ment, people are feasting on the streets, studying for exams, or singing ballads in KTVs. Somewhere a woman with a modest salary is buying ten-thousand-yuan pants from Chloé to prove her worth. Even though I couldn't cut it at the Beijing Film Academy, I knew the city itself was for me. The dinosaur bones found underneath shopping malls, the peony gardens, the enclaves of art—these things were all exhilarating for me. I walk through new commercial complexes constructed at Guomao, which look at once like big awkward gangsters gawking at one another, as if hesitant to offer one another cigarettes, and I think, I belong here.

Tonight, somehow I end up crawling out of a cab to throw up by the side of the freeway. Traffic swirls around me even though the morning light's not fully up. Then out of the blue, Sara and Benji appear, apparently because they happened to see my big head with the grooved patterns shaved into it projectile-vomiting as their cab was passing. They pat me on the back and we eat hot pot on the side of the road from an old Xin Jiang lady. I am so happy to be with them. It's at this moment I realize that what's going on is already slipping away, and while the cool air blows against my damp face in the taxi home, I can't help but miss it already.

One night, my last real girlfriend He Jing calls me.

She says, "I'm moving to Shanghai next month, and I'm wondering if you could lend me some money to get settled. You know I'm good for it." She knows more about me than anyone and there's not even a hiccup of hesitation in her voice.

That's just how He Jing did things, the girl couldn't just sit on a chair, she had to lie in it, with her head cocked to the side and a cigarette dangling dangerously. She is a sound mixer I met at the academy and always dressed as if she had a Harley parked out back. Her playground was Mao's Live House, where she rejoiced in the last blaze of China's metalhead scene.

There was never going to be a future for us, my father would never have accepted a poor musician into the family. Yet it was she who dumped me, simply saying, "I wish I could give you more, you should have more."

I meet her for coffee and hand her an envelope of money and she accepts it as though it's a book or a CD. She has cut her hair like a boy but is still fiercely radiant with confidence.

"We're doing well, you know," I say. "Benji's trying to get British art dealers to buy his photographs and Sara's in talks with a Dutch museum to exhibit her media installation. And Gangzi just got published in a Finnish fashion magazine."

She goes, "That's impressive, but what are you doing?"

My throat is dry, and I'm not sure what to say, so I go, "I'm in between projects."

"Right," she says, reaching over and messing up my hair.

Gangzi's relationship with Zi Yang isn't exactly normal either. Two days after they met, she moved into his room and began spending all her time in his bed. It is so weird in there even the pets stay away. For one, she would walk around topless, one minute laughing, the next waking us up with bawls.

"That girl should be taking antidepressants," Sara said.

In the mornings Zi Yang tells Gangzi she loves him and he believes it. In the afternoons she says he is disgusting to her and he believes that, too. "You can't just pick and choose," he tells us. "When you're trying to get someone to love you, you have to take everything." When she sleeps with him, he marvels at all the soft places on her body he can kiss. It amazes him how easily he bruises when she kicks him away.

Gangzi's website quickly becomes a shrine to Zi Yang's face. She is so crazy it's as if she stole his eyes and hung them above her at all times. Gone are all the projects he's been working on and we hardly see him without her. It is only Zi Yang, her in the bathtub with goldfish, her on his bed with broken liquor bottles, lovingly captured and rendered over and over again.

We send one another his links over QQ. "This is kind of obsessive," JJ types.

"It's just a major muse mode," responds Benji as he leans over to kiss Sara behind her ear.

More than anyone, Sara is the woman who helped all of us get over our shyness with and general distrust of white people. With Sara we learned many of her American customs, like hugging, and that took months of practice. "Arms out, touch face, squeeze!" We learned that Americans are able to take certain things for granted, such as the world appreciating their individuality. That they were raised believing they were special, loved, and that their parents wanted them to follow their dreams and be happy. It was endlessly amazing.

We also learned English. We realized how different it really was to speak Chinese. We didn't used to have to say what we meant, because our old language allows for a certain amount of wiggle room.

In Chinese we can ask, "What's it like?" because "it" can

refer to anything going on, anything on your mind. The answer could be as simple sounding as the one-syllable "men," which means that you're feeling stifled but lonely. The character drawn out is a heart trapped within a doorway. Fear is literally the feeling of whiteness. The word for "marriage" is the character of a woman and the character of fainting. How is English, that clumsy barking, ever going to compare?

But learn we did, expressions like "Holy shit" and useful acronyms like DTF (Down to Fuck), and we also became really good at ordering coffee. We learned how to throw the word "love" around, say "LOL," and laugh without laughing.

That afternoon, I buy He Jing a parting present at an outdoor flea market. A *guoguo,* a pet katydid in a woven bamboo orb. They were traditionally companion pets for lonely old men, and the louder their voice, the more they were favored. He Jing picks out a mute one. The boy selling it to me says it will live for a hundred days.

"A hundred days?" she says as she brings the woven bamboo orb up against her big eyes. "This wee trapped buddy is going to rhyme its own pitiful song for a hundred whole days?"

I tell her, "That's not so long, it's the length of summer in Beijing. That's the length of a love affair." I realize I am giving away all my secrets. I think, I want to roll you into the crook of my arm and take you somewhere far and green. When she turns back toward me, I know the answer to my question before I even ask it. I realize it is a mistake, the gesture, everything about me. She isn't going anywhere with me.

The only thing I have to offer her is money, and she has it

already. I want to tell her that there's a lot of good shit about me that she would miss out on. But there's no art in me and she sees it plainly in front of her. Instead I kiss her fingers goodbye. They smell like cigarettes and nail polish, and I swear I'll never forget it.

By autumn, the trees shiver off their leaves and Zi Yang, too, becomes frigid and bored with Gangzi. Our old friend Xiu Zhu comes back from "studying" abroad in Australia. She is a rich girl who looks like a rich boy. She has a crew cut, taped-up breasts, and an Audi TT, which she drives with one muscular arm on the steering wheel. Within an hour of meeting Zi Yang, we can all tell that she is stealing her. By the time they finish their first cocktail, Xiu Zhu is already whispering English love songs into Zi Yang's ear.

We see less and less of Gangzi after that. He still hangs out with both of them, going to lesbian *lala* bars and getting hammered. The girls hold hands and laugh while he drinks whiskey after whiskey. He mournfully watches them kiss as if he's witnessing an eclipse. A group of confused lesbians politely ask where he got such a successful gender reassignment surgery and he drinks until he passes out.

For my part, my father stops writing me emails asking about my well-being and just sends me a plane ticket. I don't tell anyone, but I go to get my visa picture taken. The agency makes me take my earring out. Within the hour, the hole closes and now it's just a period of time manifested as a mole.

· · ·

In winter, Zi Yang moves back to Hong Kong and breaks two hearts. Shortly after that, Gangzi packs up his things as well. He tells us that under Beijing, beneath the web of shopping malls and housing complexes, lay the ruins of an ancient and desolate city. And beneath that there are two rivers, one that flows with politics and one that flows with art. If you drift here, you must quench your thirst with either of its waters, otherwise there is no way to sustain a life.

"I realize there is nothing for me here," he says, "no love, not for a guy like me. It's waiting for me back in Wenzhou, that's where it must be."

He sells his cameras, his clothes, even his cellphone.

"I don't want to leave a road to come back by," he says.

We all take him to the train station where he is leaving with the same grade-school backpack he arrived with. It's as if a spell has broken and suddenly we feel like jokers in our preripped jeans and purple Converses. We remember years ago, after having borrowed money from relatives, those first breaths taken inside that station. How timidly we walked forward with empty pockets and thin T-shirts. We had been *tu*, dirt, Chinese country bumpkins. And now one of us was giving up, but what could we have said to convince him he was wrong? What could have made him stay?

Everyone on the platform has his or her own confession to make, but when we open our mouths, the train arrives, just in time to keep our shameful secrets to ourselves. Someone is about to give away the mystery of loneliness and then the train comes. A reason for living, the train comes, why she never loved him, the train comes, source of hope, train, lifetime of regret, train, never-ending heartache, train, train, train, train, train.

Afterward we huddle inside the station's Starbucks, quietly sipping our macchiatos. Our cigarette butts are swept up by street sweepers whose weekly salaries probably amounted to what we paid for our coffee. The misty mournful day is illuminated by the pollution that makes Beijing's light pop, extending the slow orange days.

Out of nowhere JJ says, "I'm not sure if I actually like drinking coffee."

Sara says something about leaving soon to go home, and from the look on Benji's face it is clear to me that this time she might not be returning.

I want to say that I might be leaving, too, but instead I focus on an American couple sitting across the room from us. The woman holds in her arms a baby who doesn't look anything like her. They are an older couple, ruddy-cheeked and healthy, and they order organic juice and cappuccinos in English. As we sit together in those chairs, their Chinese baby starts screaming and banging his juice on the table. The couple is starting to look despondent. The woman catches us staring, and the four of us look encouragingly at the baby. It's going to be okay, Chinese baby. You're a lucky boy. Such a lucky boy. Now please, please, shut up, before the Americans change their mind and give you back.

· · ·

We somehow finish the Brass Donkey video and it's a semipornographic piece of garbage that gets banned immediately, of course. The band is happy because they're stamping "Banned in China" on their CDs and are being invited on a European tour. Without telling my friends I go to the embassy to pick up my visa, secretly building the bridge on which to leave them. As I get out of there, I push back swarms of shabbily dressed Chinese people just trying to get a glimpse of America, and it makes me feel lightheaded with good fortune.

The crowded scene reminds me of waiting at the ferry docks when I was a little boy, before my father had any money. Our region was very hilly and in order to get any kind of shopping done, we took ferries to reach the nearest shops. The rickety boats were always so overcrowded and flimsy that they would regularly tip over into the river, spilling both young and old into the river's green waters. What I remember most were those brief moments of ecstasy, when the small, overloaded boat gave in and the waters were met with high-pitched screams. And we'd all swim to shore, resigned to and amused by our rotten luck. Everybody would then simply get on another boat dripping with water, letting our wet clothes dry in the breeze.

Brass Donkey's now-banned song is playing loudly in my head. It's actually pretty good, a protest song hiding behind a disco beat. "We have passion, but do not know why. What are we fighting for? Where is our direction? Do you want to be an individual? Or a grain of sand."

White Tiger of the West

THERE'S A SAYING that goes "When you're young you shouldn't read *Journey to the West,* and when you're old it's best to tuck away *Romance of the Three Kingdoms.*" In the autumn of your life, you wouldn't want to be plagued by the worries and regrets of five lifetimes. For those delicate adolescent days, the fabled feats of *Journey* would make you too dreamy; you would think yourself reckless, more powerful than you really are. You'd ride your bicycle into the sky and hop like the Monkey King through peach-shaped clouds and into another more magical universe.

Years later, Grandmaster Tu would say *Journey* was the explanation for the six-inch-long scar across his chest. He had jumped confidently, lanky arms outstretched, off the ledge of a two-story wall onto a great tree branch that tore through him.

Presently, he no longer feels the need to defend his unrivaled control of qi, nor does he question his supernatural powers of perception. His youthful complexion is glowing; his lotus pose is in perfect harmony with the sun and the moon; and if he wants to, he can cure any diseases you might have. As a fully realized spiritual qigong grandmaster, he is no longer beguiled by fantasies meant for foolish teenagers. There is nothing about his being a higher-level immortal that he himself questions. But to prove it to the nonbelievers, the skeptics, and the uninformed, he chooses to eat glass.

In the province of Heilongjiang, in a town north of Harbin and just east of Qiqihar, lived a boy named Tutu. As a child he was short and sickly, with skin the color of peeling eucalyptus bark. Most of his youth was spent in a forgotten industrial city covered in hard sooty snow and it appeared that Tutu was on his way to becoming just another knitted cap on a dreary snowy street.

His father was a coal miner, a thin, muscular man who looked permanently charred. He returned home twice a year, and each time he would ask his son how old he was, as if he hoped the boy would perhaps magically skip a year or two without his knowing.

In trying to make himself more interesting to his father, Tutu yearned to be good at sports. He did not excel at badminton because he was too short or at soccer since he was too slow. And volleyball? Not with hands that small. Classmates and teachers had no problem not noticing him either, and thus with his ordinary face and mediocre grades, he was permanently assigned to the second-to-last row in every class.

And so the calendar moved on and Tutu inched his way toward manhood, quiet and visibly disappointed with his meager lot. In an effort to cheer him up, his well-meaning mother, Cai Xia, regularly read him newspaper articles she thought he would find encouraging.

"Look," she said. "Here's a photo of a girl around your age with no arms, playing the piano with her feet! Her feet! It says she has to hold her chopsticks with her toes!"

His mother had lived a difficult life, full of compromise and fear. She was grateful for a modest apartment and a job ripping tickets at the zoo. She had no great expectations for her son, only that his life be composed of a bit more joy, a bit less hardship than her own.

Tutu only stared intensely at the photo of the grinning, piano-playing armless girl. He stared and ate sunflower seeds, cursing his luck for having hands to eat them with.

Then a few days before his eighteenth birthday, Tutu happened to come upon a mass of people huddled together in the downtown cluster of shops. It might have been a demonstration for a local contortionist, a comedian, or perhaps a salesman selling knives that resharpen themselves. But on this afternoon there was only a scrawny boy onstage. The boy must have been even younger than he was, shorter and less handsome, and yet he held the audience captive.

"Ten years ago, I was struck with polio," the boy yelled. "The doctors said I would never walk again!"

"But look at him standing!" a man in the crowd yelled back.

"I taught myself how to heal, how to stand up, walk, even run. I learned how to do the impossible through the strength and wisdom of Qilun Gong!"

"It can't be!" the crowd replied.

"Hear my story!" the boy said as his assistants handed out pamphlets. "I can teach you to cleanse your body of its ailments. Join me, and you can improve everything you are!"

Tutu felt as if the boy were looking straight into his eyes.

"They said I'd never walk again!"

The crowd applauded and cheered.

"And yet with the teachings of the Qilun, here I stand!" The boy posed like a movie hero. He jumped up and down, and the crowd roared with applause.

As the throng gushed toward the stage to grab the brochures, Tutu hung back, watching his strong legs in the shadow on the ground. He turned around and began to run. He ran past the glass bottle factory, the soap factory, and the steaming tofu snack stalls. He ran past his elementary school, past students jumping rope, old men playing chess, and women scrubbing laundry on rocks. He ran as if he were being chased all the way back to his apartment, because he couldn't wait another minute. He ran up the stairs, through the front door, and into the bathroom. There he slammed the door and stared at his flat, pimpled face in the mirror.

There were many selves that belonged to him, existing simultaneously. There was a self he knew he was, a self he wished he was, and a self he was going to be. All of these possible Tutus presented themselves to him and he realized he could choose beyond them all. A rebirth. Like the boy who told people that he shouldn't be able to walk. Or the mother who lifted a two-ton truck off her child with her bare hands. The ordinary be-spectacled clerk who dared ask a goddess from the heavens for a kiss. And the general who led his troops bravely into certain death. These myths and legends always began with an uninspiring nobody—in other words, somebody just like him.

Tutu could be an ordinary boy. He could get a job at the local factory and be like one of those men who walk out of the doors each night with a small bottle of liquor knocking against his chest pocket. But as he looked at himself, his face grew hot with what he knew must be the earth's energy. A vision appeared before him, brilliant and clear. Tutu was going to master qigong, too, but he wasn't going to do it as a follower. Something amazing had to happen for that. Something incredible had to come true.

If Cai Xia were still alive today, she might not even be able to recognize her son, Grandmaster Tu. His appearance, with his smooth skin and thick caterpillar-shaped eyebrows, is one of cultivated tranquility. His unextraordinary face, suspended above a lotus, has been printed on hundreds of laminated posters. His followers say that Grandmaster Tu is the perfect balance of the fox and weasel spirits and is so completely engulfed in qi that his body's vital energy could be described as equal to that of a large flame.

Grandmaster Tu invented the White Tiger Gong. Legend has it that he can walk through walls and see in pitch darkness. He looks young because he only ages one year for every ten human years because the blood of the white tiger runs through his veins. He came up with these legends himself, so that his devoted followers could spread them by word of mouth.

Thanks to Qilun Gong, there will never be a shortage of qigong masters in China. Ordinary citizens—taxi drivers, noodle pullers, and schoolteachers—who lead hordes of elderly followers along riverbeds in public parks hoping to achieve inner peace and physical harmony. But Grandmaster Tu's ambition was far greater than the devotion of the old and feeble. He set his sights on conquering Chinese diaspora of North America.

Thirty thousand donated and borrowed yuan was paid to a travel agency to secure a tourist visa and aid him in this endeavor. Before he arrived, he placed a full-page advertisement in the most reputable Chinese-language newspaper, *China Daily*. In the brochures he planned to hand out to his potential followers, he detailed the first time he fully realized his extraordinary powers. Five years ago, when he was just eighteen, Grandmaster Tu wrestled and killed a five-hundred-pound white tiger with his bare hands. A newspaper clipping with the headline read "Boy accidentally locked inside the tiger's enclosure is found alive! Tiger dead."

But as Grandmaster Tu liked to say, the beginning is not the most important or interesting part of the story. Just exactly how he accessed his powers, superhuman strength, perceptions, and stamina is too intricate to explain. What it comes down to is this: He was one with the qi; he had it grasped within himself, like a fist around a snake's neck. If he accepted you as his pupil, he would teach you the way. And if you needed convincing, the Great Spiritual United States Los Angeles Qigong Conference with Grandmaster Tu was coming up in a public arena on Main Street, Alhambra, at 7 p.m. Free admission.

Of course, as with any life story of an extraordinary man, there was a woman. And in this case, she was still only a little girl.

If you happened to have visited Disneyland in the late nineties, you might have seen a crowd of eight to fifteen middle-aged Chinese businessmen dressed in dark suits following a small and serious Chinese girl with a big forehead and small feet and wearing a backpack.

That little girl was named Mary.

Housed in the employee apartment of a Super 8 motel, Mary was one-third of the Cherry Sky Travel Agency. Technically both of her parents were full-time employees of Super 8 Monterey Park, but they were also industrious new immigrants, so they ran a travel agency part-time. They were taking advantage of the import-export boom of the early nineties and catering to "research" tour groups.

When Mary's mom wasn't manning the front desk, visa paperwork and planning itineraries were her responsibilities. Mary's dad drove the agency van while also taking care of any physical labor the motel required, from declogging the toilets to ejecting unwanted guests. Mary considered herself an unofficial Cherry Sky part-timer when she wasn't attending fourth grade. She worked weekends.

Mary's job was simple. Armed with half-priced children's season passes, she guided Chinese tour groups through every theme park from Universal Studios to SeaWorld. This entailed strategic marching to the five "emblematic" spots where the tourists could take photos. She corralled them to the side when they created roadblocks, translated "How much is that?" and replied to concerns for the average American waistline or the warmth of a certain American baby not wearing a hat on a windy day. She directed the guests to bathrooms and memorized the shops with the biggest selection of souvenirs.

The customers politely offered her parents compliments about Mary: "This girl is going to be a great leader! It's amazing how mature and clever she is!"

"Aiya! This chubster? Not likely. She's no good at math!" her mom would say.

"Aiya! No such thing! Thank *you* for being so understanding about our makeshift half-squirt guide!" her dad would chime in.

Mary was a pudgy, pigeon-toed child with disproportionally large teeth, and her parents liked to bring that up, too, for laughs. She was told they all needed to make sacrifices. That's why Mary still wore the same sweat suits she brought with her from China with cartoon dogs and nonsensical English phrases on them. She used the same old blue backpack that had to be rolled on plastic wheels, so she could be heard coming down the corridors of her school long before she turned the corner.

Therefore, regardless of how clever she was with clients, she was just another F.O.B. from China in elementary school.

It had been a typical Wednesday. It was hours since the last bell and the elementary-school parking lot was nearly empty. Mary sat alone on the curb, squinting down the street for her dad's car, which was late as usual.

When she opened the door, she was surprised to find a

young man wearing a black martial-arts outfit sitting in the backseat. He sat with his palms flat against his legs and gave off a pleasant woody smell.

"Ni Ni"—her dad called her by her Chinese name from the front seat—"say hi to Uncle Tu. He is our newest guest. This is our only daughter."

"Nice to meet you, Uncle Tu," she responded.

"Uncle Tu is a qigong master—no, wait, I mean *grand*master," continued her dad, winking at her in the rearview mirror, "which means he has special powers."

Tutu didn't notice the snide comment because his mind was in another world. He had been trying to put himself at ease through breathing exercises after seeing the embarrassingly small space rented for his conference. It was just an empty office, not enough room for a large crowd. Plus it was located next door to an orthodontist's office and the sounds of screaming children leaked through the walls.

When he finally turned to glance at the little girl, he saw that she was quietly studying him. So he spoke to her. "Ni Ni, how do you like being ten?"

"How did you know how old I was?" Her eyes were wide with astonishment.

"I can just tell. It's one of my gifts."

"What else? Can you tell me another thing?" she asked. "With one of your other gifts?"

"I can tell you're part girl, part tiger," he replied calmly. "You have a girl's body but a tiger's soul." And he leaned his head over the armrest and said, "You're powerful and you are angry like the tiger within you."

"Oh, ha ha! Wow! That's unlikely because if there's one thing about Ni Ni, it's that she's the most *tinghua,* obedient," piped up her father. "No tiger here! Go on, tell Uncle Tu!"

"I have another question for you," Tutu said without waiting for Mary to react. "What is a good English name for me? I have one. It's . . . it's Jieon?"

"John?" Mary asked.

"Yes, that one. Jieon. I don't like it. It sounds like 'sauce' in Chinese. Can you think of another one for me?"

Los Angeles, City of Angels, where dreams come true. Chinese immigrants occupy another Los Angeles, and unfortunately, that's where this story is set. In the nineties, the terrified locals of Alhambra had long since fled, taking everything with them except the Denny's. Sizzler became Liu's Dumpling House, Pizza Hut became Taiwanese Beef Jerky Hut, and Mongolian Hot Pot bore the distinctive architectural flourish of Taco Bell.

The new children learned their perfect English from television. They wore shocked expressions and cheap clothes and measured popularity by the model of their parents' cars. Mary tried to make friends with the American-born girls, who were all beauties in her mind, based on the fact that they had better clothes. She spent a lot of her energy learning the ways in which they wore their hair, what music they listened to, which *Friends* character they claimed was their favorite.

There were so many unanswered questions banging around

in her mind. Like how come her dad cursed every customer behind their back but was afraid to even ask them a question? Or
when would they move out of the motel and into a real apartment? Would she ever see her old friends from kindergarten
in China again, or were they to be forgotten? On top of these
worries, there was food in the school cafeteria she didn't know
how to eat and Jehovah's Witnesses she wasn't allowed to open
the door for. Not to mention the Girl Scouts, who zealously
sold expensive cookies.

After meeting Grandmaster Tu, Mary began to realize that
maybe she *was* angry. Why did she have to sleep so early on Friday nights? She hated not being able to watch cartoons on Sat-
urdays. She hated having to translate every stupid thing anyone
wanted to say. She heard herself growling in class and began to
feel as if she were prowling the halls of her elementary school.
The day after meeting the grandmaster, while waiting for her
dad to pick her up, Mary smashed the plastic wheels of her
backpack on the curb.

Unlike other clients, Tutu didn't want his picture taken in front
of amusement park signs, nor did he want to take a bus to Las
Vegas. He wasn't even interested in going to strip clubs. Instead,
he practiced qigong on the lawn of the motel, moving invisible
boulders, holding streams between his arms.

Mary pretended to play with LEGOs on a picnic bench
while she watched him.

Like magic, he suddenly appeared by her side. "What are
you building?"

"An animal hospital. This is where the horses would lie down, and here is where the pigs get surgery and X-rays."

It wasn't actually an animal hospital, but she felt the need to impress him. In the presence of a man with special powers, she was very self-conscious about whether or not ten-year-olds could still play with LEGOs.

"Why don't you try to use all the pieces to build a tower?" he asked, touching the hard pieces between his fingers.

"That's . . . that's boring, just one tower. Why would I do that?"

"Don't you want to see how high you can get it to go? Can you touch the roof? How long do you think before you could touch the cloud?"

"Can you touch the cloud?" She gave him an expectant look.

"I can do whatever I want to," he replied. "Because I am not afraid of anything."

She raised her head toward the sky. "Can you teach me how not to be afraid of anything, too?"

"Depends on how open you are to learning." He smiled and put his hand on top of her head, where it felt hot, genuinely hot, against her hair. "I've already begun teaching you. Are you paying attention?" he said. By the time her head felt the normal temperature again, she realized he had gone back to his position and resumed meditating.

As soon as Grandmaster Tu was out of earshot, Mary's dad walked out from the office where he was working. "Don't listen to anything that hack says," he told Mary. "He's just here to swindle people out of their hard-earned money."

· · ·

At night in his room, Tutu hardly slept. He was preparing himself in anticipation of the upcoming conference. He studied the books *Dao* and *Tu Qin Xia* and cultivated his qi cross-legged in the dark. Shivering with knowing and calm, he felt he was becoming one of the gods.

The day of his big event, Grandmaster Tu woke up picturing hundreds of people lining up to kiss his hands. A terribly excited Mary knocked on his door, and together he and the entire family piled into their purple minivan and pulled into the parking lot.

Five men were waiting. They looked skeptical and they looked poor.

Without a moment's pause, Grandmaster Tu made his way across the parking lot and entered into the back room. Mary followed him, skipping to keep up.

"I am not nervous, but could you please bring me some water?" he asked her as he walked through the door.

The plain room was set up with chairs lining the walls. As the time got closer to seven, the chairs filled, even if some of the attendees were just people who had wandered in from the street.

Mary was happy for him; she interpreted the change in his voice as the force of qi turning on like a motor. To make sure she got the best view, she sat on a box of office supplies, high off the ground. She was eager for the grandmaster to prove himself, for what she was about to see. Was he going to levitate above a lotus blossom? Was he going to walk through a wall?

Tutu walked into the room wearing his martial-arts outfit. "I am Grandmaster Tu," he announced, then paused and added,

"English name Danny. The spiritual master of China, hailing from the northeast."

"You are in the presence of a Taoist immortal. I harnessed the energy of the moon through the coal-smacked skies. When I killed a white tiger as a young boy, I came alive."

He began to circle the room, holding a half-filled glass of water in front of him.

"I will use my qi to soften this glass to water. It will cower and become unable to cut me."

He flicked the glass with his fingers, producing that familiar *clink*. He passed it and encouraged people in the room to do the same.

"Do not try this yourself. Only when your gong has achieved the highest cultivation will you be able to do this on your own."

Mary stared at the drinking glass she'd handed to him just moments earlier. It was clear and fairly tall, with a slightly thicker bottom; they had the same glasses at home.

"Many people have hurt themselves trying to replicate my craft," he began, launching into a series of anecdotes. "There was a soldier who cut his tongue out . . ."

He encouraged the audience to be astonished. Mary shivered when picturing the bloody saliva he described, the convulsing limbs and screams of pain. She steadied her chin on top of her knee and prepared to witness a miracle.

He paused in the center of the room and stood with his feet apart and breathed heavily as his open palm applied invisible forces to the glass.

Then, just as the room was about to turn impatient, he grabbed his glass with both hands and took a bite out of it. He bit the glass as easily as one would a leaf of lettuce. Crisp and clean. The crunch of glass sounded like metal plates falling onto tile, and as he continued to chew, shards shattered all over him.

Mary looked at him and the grandmaster looked back. Time was passing by in microwave minutes, shockingly slow. Mary watched as he took another bite and chewed, the crunching sound resonating through the quiet room. He swallowed and opened his mouth so that everyone could see his tongue.

Perhaps some of the younger men in the audience had come to see this kind of bizarre spectacle, maybe hoping to be entertained by a few magic tricks. Maybe the dental assistant and the office worker thought qigong could alleviate the pain of muscle injuries and showed up to ask a grandmaster for information on alternative medicine. Yet here they were, with aching backs and damp palms, watching a young man much like themselves daring himself to eat a glass cup.

Nobody ventured to walk out of the room, and not one horrified face twisted the other way; they were locked in the trance together.

"Stop, stop, you're bleeding," said a concerned man.

"No," Tutu said, his mouth full of glass. "That's just my lips. It is unaffected by the qi; the glass is not cutting me at all."

"Really, please stop, we get it," said another.

Tutu wiped the corner of his mouth with a sleeve, smearing a few drops of blood across his cheek. Rather than stopping, he raised his hand before continuing to chew and swallow.

Finally Mary's father got up from his chair and reached out as if to take the rest of the glass from his hands. But Mary ran up and blocked her father's path, and used all her strength to settle him back down in his chair.

"No, no, please let him finish," she said. "Isn't this amazing? He's showing us what he can do!"

The whole glass disappeared into the grandmaster's mouth.

"It's a miracle!" Mary yelled, her voice going hoarse. "He proved it! He proved it!"

Unfortunately for Grandmaster Tu, even after he rinsed off his partially bloody mouth, peeled back his lips, and showed everyone his intact tongue, nobody signed up for his classes or gave him any money. The eyes of those Chinese American audience members did not fill up with wonder as he had hoped, as he had expected, but instead they shone with confusion, despair, and pity. Perhaps they were too familiar with desperate survival tactics. Maybe they were not yet looking for spiritual guidance. For whatever reason, his demonstration did not put his audience in a state of wonder. Success and failure exist side by side in Los Angeles. For every Wenzhou farmer who buys a mansion in Diamond Bar, there's another who will wash dishes until his back gives out.

When Mary tiptoed to Grandmaster Tu's room later that evening to wish him good night, he did not answer the door. The next morning his motel room was empty of all his possessions. He did not leave the rest of the money he owed to Mary's family, and on his return flight to China, his was the only empty seat. Her parents said that nobody had seen him leave; it was as if he simply vanished.

In the years to come, Mary would remember Grandmaster

Tu spontaneously, with a kind of baffled veneration. He would appear to her like a pebble dropped into still water, during strange moving moments that she could not explain. When she hitchhiked through Argentina as a teenager. When she whipped through the streets of Lisbon on the back of a retro scooter. Or when on a rainy morning in Italy the ringing of church bells moved her to tears. Her parents never did figure out when or why the obedient daughter they raised grew stiff wings and flew far away from them. When, in her most glorious moments, she fought for herself and claimed what was hers, she would anticipate his memory.

It had been printed in the newspapers that an old and alcoholic guard had forgotten to lock a door to the tiger's sanctuary and a young boy accidentally entered the enclosure. A Siberian beast against a powerless lamb. This was a fabrication, because the boy knew exactly what he was doing the evening he entered the caged jungle with his stolen key. His mother had told him there was a tiger, holding on for weeks now, waiting to be put down.

The big cat's pupils were thick and unseeing. Its wasted body sensed the boy's presence. When the boy approached the tiger, it could not even rise; it roared weakly at the boy, showing its one yellow tooth.

Under the moon, like a brush lifting out of the ink, the tiger stood to face the boy. The night was hushed. Even in its broken state, the creature was still graceful, its shoulders powerful; the Han character for king, written by the gods long before time, spread darkly above its gray eyes.

The tiger swayed. It had been trapped for twenty years in its cage, had never known anything but this prison. It yearned for death. The boy drew closer, crouching with his thin arms by his sides, one hand brandishing a pocketknife like a sword.

On its hind legs, the tiger was twice the height of the boy, and the first time its claws came down, the boy's head spilled blood in a stream behind his ears. Yet the boy lunged with the knife at the tiger's throat and tumbled into its claws. When the tiger began to tire, the boy attacked again. This final time he climbed behind the tiger and stabbed at its throat with his only miserable weapon. The tiger, ivory in the moonlight, rolled its deep mountain song in its mouth but could not, or perhaps did not want to, shake off the boy.

There are few certainties in life. That the nights would be dark and that the sun would rise in the east every morning, these things the boy took for granted. In the morning, he thought, he would be reborn a legend in this gray world. He knew that to be extraordinary, first there must be courage. For people to follow him, he had to descend upon a road to lead them on.

For Our Children and for Ourselves

IN A BLUE sky smeared with white clouds, his mother's pigeons whirled above his head in enormous sweeps. This household chore was one he never grew tired of. He tended daily to the birds, encouraged them, and as they dove their wings took on every shade of gray. These were kites people could never dream of, he thought, and as they weaved in and out between those old porcelain roof tiles and plum trees, they drew invisible watercolors and characters without names.

With a loud thud, Xiao Gang slapped the long branch he was waving against the tree trunk. The pigeons continued to fly on their own. A few plums fell to the ground, and boys from the neighborhood scrambled to pick them up. "Mine! Mine!" they shouted.

When they were too tired to fly, the pigeons one by one

settled back into their hutches, puffed out their feathers, and cooed gently in unison, like heartbeats slowing down to slumber. A child from the city might ask why none of them ever flew away into the inviting mountains and trees in the distance. But this was the Henan countryside, where that would be a stupid question.

On this particular night, Xiao Gang was looking to get very, very drunk. He wanted to be carried home singing. As the occasion was his bachelor party, all of his buddies—booze in hand, undershirts already stained from spills—were ready to fulfill his wish.

After the fish was picked to bones, Liang stood up unsteadily and raised his brimming glass of *baijiu* to give a toast. "To your journey, brother!" Cheers were grunted, lips smacked, and cigarettes lit.

"Ever since we were this tall"—Liang gestured with his fat hands at his hips—"we've been best friends, and maybe not by blood but I always saw you as my brother. And if I can't speak to you from the gut, then who can, huh?"

Xiao Gang looked at him, smiled sloppily, and filled his own cup.

"To this lucky bastard, he's going to get rich in America!"

Surrounded by his closest friends, Xiao Gang cheered with them.

"Your wife," Liang continued, "well, your wife is . . ." He looked around, as if searching for a euphemism, then he shouted, "Your wife is a retard!"

The snickering around the table stopped, a series of throats cleared. Someone's arm gently went around Liang's meaty shoulders.

But Liang continued, his eyes beginning to swim in their puffy alcohol pools. "Ah, but her mom's got money! And she ain't stingy!

"Brother, you're gonna live far better than us losers! Damn it all, let's *ganbei* to that!" Without waiting for anyone else, Liang threw his head back, gulped his shot, and held his glass upside down above his head.

Xiao Gang searched the faces of his closest friends for pity or jealousy, but none returned his gaze. Except for Liang, who reached out and put an arm around him. This was the man he'd fought with as a teenager, with whom he shared everything he'd ever had. Xiao Gang grabbed him roughly by the collar and kissed him on the cheek.

Their friends laughed, showing their crowded, yellowing teeth. They clinked their glasses and then *baijiu*, that clear warm venom, burned their throats.

"*Gong xi!*" they yelled. "Congratulations!" in a tone no different than if he'd won the lottery.

Liang drifted away from the group, slumped in a chair, and began drinking alone. He worked at a paper factory, and though he was only twenty-eight, he was already wearing old-man shoes. The winter winds had etched deep grooves into his cheeks long before the years could get to them.

He and Xiao Gang could have had a real heart-to-heart that night and gotten things straight before the spell of their friendship was irreparably broken, but not knowing the words, they drank instead, until they had nothing to say at all.

. . .

Whether he believed it or not, about six months ago, Xiao Gang had tumbled helplessly into the grasp of *yuan fen*. The term *yuan* means the fateful meeting of two people, with the possibility—the shared hope—of becoming love. *Fen* was the responsibility of fulfilling that unspoken promise. *Yuan* and *fen* make love stories possible.

Yuan—not quite fate—had been at work giving birth to the millions of invisible strings that pulled Xiao Gang, a single-winged seed from the Henan countryside, to his current situation. When he packed his bags for the last time and walked the long road to where a car waited to pick him up, that was *fen*, propelling him toward the realization of that destiny.

Three weeks before his twenty-eighth birthday, Xiao Gang was engaged to an American girl he'd never met. The connection took only a single moment. The world turned as always, a sugar cube lost itself in tea, train stations united lovers, corn grew golden, and kites went up in the air. In this moment, *yuan fen* grabbed hold of Xiao Gang, counted his steps, and drew his hand to the door he held open for Vivian, the mother of his future wife.

After that, everything changed.

Vivian Tang's favorite topic of conversation was money. Mortgage rates, import taxes. Her most uttered sentences included "Oh, this thing? My personal shopper at Neiman picked it out. It's a special order from Milan." She wore nothing but Italian suits, tailored to hug her short, stocky frame. For the past two decades she had worn her hair in a poufy bun of tight curls, dyed deep maroon, high on the back of her head.

She had been married only once, in her twenties, when she still lived in China. But whenever her husband gave her that tragic look of his and delivered in cadenced sighs his juvenile overtures about love, she had changed the subject to the more practical matters at hand—where they would go to graduate school, when they would be able to buy an apartment, the rising price of pork. So she wasn't surprised, some years later, when she realized he had stopped bringing up the subject of love. And she was not greatly disappointed when, soon after they immigrated to America and their daughter was born, he left her for someone else. Vivian did not mourn his loss; she did not want to resemble her weak and unfocused husband. Just by looking at the back of her head, people knew she was tough. The tight cluster of dyed curls spoke of a woman who did not have time for mood lighting and poetry, someone who took pride in never having loved her husband.

Yong Qin was her Chinese name. She knew that those characters did not convey any elegance, but she'd always felt the name directly represented her personal virtues: bravery and hard work. Every day she forced herself out of bed, to her desk, and eventually into business school in Massachusetts. Most people were so intimidated by the fierce clarity with which she spoke that they hardly noticed the accent that still clung to her words. Within a decade she had become a successful apparel supplier, through years of never doubting her instincts. Her company, Vivian Inc., was a major client of Xiao Gang's employer, a fabric-dyeing plant in Shenzhen.

Like the other children in the village, Xiao Gang attended a trade school and got a job in a factory. Every summer he went home to work the wheat harvest, and this would go on until he had children of his own to send out to the machines. His life stretched out before him, long and predictable. Day after day, dyeing equipment breathed hot air into his face as he lifted and loaded weave combs. There had been times when he felt a pinprick of envy that the fabric would travel to places that he could only dream of.

When he first saw this woman walking down the hall, the unfurling of her clothes and her entourage of assistants, he was in awe of her. To say she had an air of authority would have been an understatement; to Xiao Gang, she might as well have floated by on the shoulders of a hundred men. As she passed, he caught a hint of her perfume, and before the scent could leave him, her personal secretary had already caught up to him and, to his amazement, asked him to dinner.

Vivian needed only two minutes to take stock of Xiao Gang, but she saw him instantly for what he was: a slightly above-average young man with big dreams but nothing to show for them. He was a fairly tall and insignificantly handsome mid-level manager who wasn't extraordinary in any visible way. But when he held the door open for her, she sensed a rare quality in him, which she couldn't place until later. She knew right then that he was still a boy, earnest and artless, and more than that, she knew he was what she was looking for.

That night at dinner Vivian offered him a job and a U.S. green card. Under one condition.

"Her name is Melanie, and she is a very sweet girl."

. . .

He had been resigned to becoming exactly the kind of man his mother had said he would be: strong-bodied and stable-minded. When he was younger, he'd had more outlandish hopes: He had wanted to play the piano, like on the Mozart tape his neighbor sometimes played. When college exams came up, he fantasized about applying to music school. In the end, a factory job appeared and a piano didn't. His fingers grew thick and stiff before they were ever taught to follow music. As he got older, these realities became more apparent and easier to accept. Sooner or later, he figured, life rubs smooth everyone's edges.

That didn't mean he hadn't harbored the hope that somehow he would get the opportunity to live someone else's life. On his daily bus rides, he imagined the life of a millionaire businessman, millionaire rock star, millionaire government official. He wanted to be someone who saw the ocean from the sky.

Then, suddenly, the chance was here, so real he could pound his fists against it. Without needing much convincing, he agreed to meet her.

Melanie was, in fact, very sweet. Even her hairdresser said so when she untangled her long curls and permed it per Vivian's directions. Melanie loved to wear only one dress, which was the color of tangerines. She was going to wear it when she went to meet her future husband, and her mother promised that he would be "very, very nice to her."

How nice? As nice as her puppy, her music teacher, a bubble bath, as nice as playing ball at the beach, she had told herself.

Melanie had never wanted a husband, but she was thirty years old, and that's the age when her mom said every girl gets one. She thought having a husband might be like having a friend over all the time. When she was younger she had lots of friends—Sean, Taylor, Ciarra—but she had stopped going to school and didn't see them anymore.

"Please sit still, I might accidentally cut you," the hairdresser hissed.

Melanie stopped herself from rocking and looked down. Her future husband lived in China, and China was a long plane ride away. Her mother was taking her to meet him and so she got to wear her favorite dress. Red flowers were stitched on its sleeves and the flowers matched the color of her lipstick. She felt unusually pretty the day she got on the plane to go to China to meet her future husband.

Before she left, Vivian gave Xiao Gang the keys to her Shanghai apartment. For a week, as he waited for Vivian to return with his bride, he was lost in a happy stupor. He'd never imagined a more amazing city, never been surrounded by so much luxury. Money she'd given him flowed out of his hands and manifested itself in the form of expensive clothes and lavish meals. He was so thrilled to be a part of this new world that he didn't think too much about the bargain, the costs of this life.

He often stayed in and sat smoking on the balcony that overlooked Shanghai Pudong. The view was magnificent, millions of lights shimmering and reflecting off the ocean that enveloped it. The traffic swirled neon ribbons underneath the Bund and he was sure that he was witnessing the future. The sight was so glorious that he ached, knowing he'd soon have to leave it behind.

Xiao Gang noticed her hand first on their official "date." Her left hand curved in above her wrist, fingers shrunken and pressed together like a broken toy. She tried to hide it in the sleeve of her dress, which was billowy but still revealed the chubby figure she had inherited from Vivian. Then he noticed her eyes, which were large, round, and calm. Finally he saw her broad, flattened forehead, which spelled out her condition for anyone who looked at her. Her mother led her by the elbow when they walked into the restaurant.

"Hello, Xiao Gang, nice to meet you, I'm Melanie," she said too loudly, as if she had rehearsed it all afternoon. From around the restaurant, her pitched voice drew stares, which lingered on her before each pair of eyes shifted away, the way eyes do when they register pity. She didn't notice any of this as she extended her perfect right hand, and he took it gently into his.

Xiao Gang looked nervously at Vivian. She had told him that Melanie was different, shy, and not like other girls, but he wasn't at all prepared for this. She was thirty, hardly a girl, but she still looked like a child whose gray hairs served to remind the world that nobody escapes age. The revulsion he felt for her drew a grimace to his face. He forced a smile at Melanie and then quickly looked away.

They sat down and ordered tea. Vivian lit a cigarette for Xiao Gang and handed it to him. For a moment, she wanted to tell him everything. How she had achieved every success she'd ever wanted, except for a perfect daughter. She wanted to confess about all the doctors she'd flown Melanie to see and the grief she felt to see her daughter stay a child forever. She wanted to say that she knew she'd owe him for the rest of her life and she would never forget it. As his mother-in-law, she would gladly give him anything he wanted in California, because he was perhaps more for herself than for Melanie. As a mother, she wanted him, to adore and take pride in as if he were her own son.

But, of course, she wouldn't allow any of that to be said. Instead she lit her own cigarette and slowly blew out the smoke.

Vivian smiled. "If you agree, we can start the paperwork on Friday."

In many ways, Xiao Gang had a lot in common with Melanie. Secretly, he, too, was easily disturbed and didn't quite fit into his surroundings. Over beers with his buddies, he could talk about women and rock and roll, but he could never tell them what he dreamed about at night.

He was always dreaming about bees.

Once, an old man who lived alone in Xiao Gang's village had raised great hives of honeybees. As a boy, Xiao Gang used to wander into that forbidden corner and watch him. He didn't remember if the old man ever spoke, or what he even looked like, only that, when alone, he was covered in bees, a constellation of gold stars sparkling over his entire body.

Years later, while Xiao Gang was working in the factory, the old man died. For almost a week, no one noticed his absence. Over time, the old man's house became abandoned and ruined. The bees he had raised became wild bees; they flew across the river and disappeared over the mountains. Yet every autumn Xiao Gang would return to his old hiding spot to await their inevitable return. He was their witness. He knew the bees would find their way back to the old man's house because they missed him.

Seeing those bees gave Xiao Gang, the son of a long line of farmers who didn't want to be farmers, a hint of some unmentioned magic in life, something he'd never dared to tell anyone.

Across the table, Melanie fiddled with her sparkly watch, which was studded with real diamonds. Her mother had told her not to pick at it, she remembered. When her future husband came to live with them, her mom would buy him presents, too. Why was he shaking like that? she wondered. He reminded her of her cat when it was startled. So Melanie hummed to Xiao Gang under her breath quietly, the way her teacher, Mrs. Medrano, had taught her that whales do. Whales sang when they were too far away from one another. That way they wouldn't feel so alone. "It's okay," she hummed over and over again.

A painful heaviness drifted up from Xiao Gang's stomach, and when he was afraid he would suffocate, he took a sharp breath. "Does she speak Chinese?" he finally asked.

"Not as well as English," Vivian said, "but she can understand most of it." She patted Melanie's wrist. "You're pretty smart, aren't you, *baobeir*?"

Melanie nodded enthusiastically.

"Ask her something, go ahead."

Xiao Gang paused for a moment, then wiped his mouth with his palm. "Is America really beautiful?"

Melanie nodded again and cackled. How nice his voice is! she thought, liking him right then. Why? Two big soft eyes, and they were smiling at her. Maybe he would agree to take her to the beach. His hands were warm and so much bigger than hers, and thinking about them touching hers, she cackled again. Oh, and he was tall. She felt a warmth inside of her chest; she was smiling inside and out.

Vivian talked about life in California, how polite and orderly the freeways were, the sky was blue every day, a satisfying variety of Chinese restaurants, and statuesque palm trees that leaned to the east. They had cars for him to drive, a desk at the office to work at; she guaranteed that he was going to be pleased with his life.

Xiao Gang nodded, but somewhere along the line he stopped listening. Instead he remembered the hands of the first girl he'd ever wanted to marry, the local snack-shop owner's daughter. In elementary school he'd expressed his feelings for her by throwing a worm into her hair or flicking mud at her. But somehow she liked him back and looked at him with eyes that made him flush down to his knees. He'd kissed her only once, when they were teenagers perched on top of boxes of noodles, his hand fumbling underneath her bra. That summer she left, like so many girls he knew. She went to college in Beijing, and he never dared to try to kiss her again.

Vivian finished her speech with a question and he nodded just in time. He turned and looked at Melanie, and her innocent expression calmed him. Vivian ordered the two of them to sit together at the table so that she could take a picture, and he put his arm around Melanie's soft shoulders. He noted how adorable she was. She reminded him of his niece. His future wife wasn't going to make him feel worthless—she was going to be pleased with him. With her, he was never going to be made to feel like a poor country fool again. He smiled gratefully for the winking camera.

Turning his head to one side, he cracked his neck bones. Perhaps she was like a business deal that he could invest a few years of his life in and then move on. With her he could finally buy things he'd always wanted, women included. These opportunities don't come every day, he thought. If Vivian wanted it, he could keep his eyes closed and put a baby into Melanie. He could do that.

He remembered the life in Shenzhen he never had to see again. He could picture himself picking at the mold that grew on his clothes in the summer, born from the dampness of his cramped company apartment, the long bus rides through dusty roads, the pile of wheat he slept on to guard it during harvest, and the persistent hum of the factory machines that drove itself into his every waking moment. The practiced motions of lifting fabrics and checking the balance of colors would take longer to forget.

Only a poor country fool would give up an opportunity like this, he thought. He reached for Melanie's hand again and held her soft childish palm in his. She gazed at him with the eyes of a kitten. He looked at Vivian. His voice shaking with something that was not quite guilt he pronounced the three English words he'd been rehearsing all afternoon: "We get married."

· · ·

To make the engagement official, Vivian had flown his mother to Shanghai, and she put all of them up in a hotel with more fountains than he'd ever seen. His mother, in her typical fashion, barely spoke.

Xiao Gang was his nickname. His mother had given it to him. It literally meant "little steel," a symbol of strength and endurance. His brothers and sisters received similar unromantic monikers and with these names became practical daughters and obedient sons.

His mother told only one story about her past. It was about Xiao Gang's older brother, on the day he went swimming in the river and never came back. How he had looked up at her, his grubby hands outstretched, and asked for three cents to buy a slice of watermelon and she had not given it to him. She told the story more often as she got older. It got longer and she would cry before she was finished. It was the only sign of tenderness Xiao Gang ever saw from her.

During a dinner of abalone steak at a restaurant with gold-plated walls, Melanie sat between Xiao Gang and Vivian and across from his mother. She smiled dutifully at the old woman, who avoided looking at her. She rocked back and forth in her chair, tracing her fingers along the carvings of her chopsticks. Xiao Gang picked them up every time she brushed them onto the floor.

Vivian leaned in close to his mother and repeated the same plan, with greater enthusiasm this time. Xiao Gang was going to have a luxury car, a position in her company, and a three-thousand-square-foot house.

"He can go swimming and bowling!" Melanie interrupted. She wanted to say something perfect for this new lady. She rounded the Os the way her speech teacher said she should. She waited in vain for a compliment from her mother.

Vivian stood up and raised her glass. "A toast to a happy marriage. Thank you for raising such a fine and capable son." She tilted her head back and the *baijiu* followed.

Xiao Gang's mother smiled awkwardly and bobbed her head up and down in agreement. "Thank you, Mrs. Tang" was the only thing she managed to say.

Every time Vivian looked at the old woman, she felt a pain that echoed its way from the memories she'd long tried to forget. Melanie as a baby, small and perfect against her breast, as if everything in life had led her to that moment. How the baby's smiles had compelled her to drop her schoolwork just so she could knit her daughter a sock. Then, as Melanie got older, she watched the faces of friends morph from joy to pity; their cheers of congratulations became muted whispers when she entered the room. She looked at Melanie and felt a tenderness that would never leave, no matter how imperfect her daughter was.

Seeing the old woman reminded her that being a mother was so difficult, that you love a child more than yourself, that you want to give the child more than you have. This is what we've got, she thought, only this endless wanting, for our children and for ourselves. She vowed to do her best—to provide everyone at the table with something to be happy about.

.   .   .

Xiao Gang loved his mother more than anyone else. She had not said to him, nor hinted even once during the return flight, the short train ride, and the long bus ride back, that maybe he didn't need to do this. Had she voiced any hesitation, said he could find his way on his own, find a pretty girl whom he loved, and make himself into a success, he knew he wouldn't have gone through with it.

Instead, his mother had packed his clothes for him, made all his favorite foods for dinner, and patted his hand before he set out for America. She was illiterate, so she wouldn't be able to write to him. She worshipped no gods, so she couldn't even pray. She let him go to be the husband of a rich girl with Down syndrome and never once wept for him.

On the day of his departure, neighbors gathered outside the front yard to watch him drag out his two meager suitcases. His dog barked, running from one corner to the other, the dirt swirling around his feet. Liang gave him a bottle of good *baijiu* he'd been hiding for years. His sister handed him her baby, whose dirty butt poked through his split-crotched pants and rested on the forearm of Xiao Gang's new coat.

Vivian's big black sedan swept right through the alleys into his front yard; neighborhood children ran after it with sticks, screaming with glee. He could feel everything—the pigeons cooing, the sunflowers turning toward the sky, the day gray with solemn clouds. With swift motions, the driver dumped the luggage into the trunk, the sedan's door closed heavily, and suddenly all was quiet and still. Xiao Gang craned his neck to look back. Through the tinted windows he could see his mother and sister. They waved.

As he watched every street he'd known pass by his window as the car wove its way out of the village, he thought about taking some pictures with his phone. Instead, because he couldn't contain himself, he began to narrate village stories to the driver.

"Here is where the butcher said he saw the dragon fall out of the sky. Now I know that man and he's never told a lie in all his life. He said it was gold, bright, the size of a goat!" He slid across the backseat and pointed out the other window.

"Oh, and do you see that miniature pagoda across the river? That's where the old ladies go to pray for rain when we have a drought. I saw it work once, too! Oh, man, I almost cried. But get this, after a few drops, the rain just stopped!"

Xiao Gang's phone rang and he saw that the caller was Vivian. For a moment he was terrified something had gone wrong. He put the phone to his ear and answered cautiously.

"Xiao Gang, listen," Vivian said. "Some things are easier to say on the phone."

He shifted nervously and wiped his sweaty palms on his pants.

"People are just animals onto which society imposes unnecessary responsibilities. Like you're supposed to have a passion and philosophize about the 'meaning' in life. Right?"

"Believe me, it's bullshit," she continued. "Nothing about this is natural. The world tortures this out of all of us. Meaning is completely unnecessary when all a human being really needs to do is live and procreate."

She paused. "Pain comes with everything else that requires

insight into humanity. A conscience is what invites trouble. Listen to me, Xiao Gang. If you keep this in mind, life is really quite simple."

He coughed, confused. "Why are you telling me this?"

She sighed, and he could tell by her voice that her eyes were watery. "Because I want you to feel satisfied with your choice. You should feel good about it. I want all of us to feel really good about this. Do you understand?"

"*Hao* . . . yes . . . y-yes," he stuttered, and then, "You don't have to worry about me, mother-in-law."

As he flipped the phone off, he stretched his back against the seat and lit a cigarette. His thoughts now swarmed all over the place. He pictured American girls with big breasts and strawberry-blond hair. He pictured Melanie's innocent child smile and broken hand, and shuddered at the thought of how it would feel against his bare thigh. He closed his eyes and for a moment felt himself covered with the old man's bees, those old friends, as if they were trying to lift him off the seat, out the window, and back to the soil where they were born. They glistened over his body like fireworks. He pressed his eyelids tightly together, and he eventually dozed off. When he opened them, he was at the airport terminal; one by one the bees disappeared, like the dew drying on a leaf.

When the flight attendant bent down to secure his seat belt, he studied her exquisite face, held smooth and still with makeup, and Xiao Gang suddenly felt panic.

He fidgeted with the buckle of his belt. The cloth of the seat cover made the back of his neck itch. He studied the fine curve of the plane's ceiling above him, three perfectly positioned features to cool him and shower him with light. He swallowed and turned to his companions.

His bride-to-be, Melanie, was slumped with her cheek against the window, already asleep, her mouth open. Her small feet were extended across his future mother-in-law's lap and onto his. He still thought of himself as Xiao Gang, but Vivian had already given him the name Travis.

The plane began to move and he jerked into an alert position. He could still change his mind; he could run away. A cold sweat passed across his forehead and he wiped it away with the back of his hand. Against every impulse of his limbs, he sat there in the seat as the plane drew its body faster and faster down the runway.

Mother, daughter, son sat still in those seats. *Yuan fen* held them together and transported them safely across the ocean. During the coming years, his nights would eventually stop being about the old man's bees, and his reveries would no longer involve pigeons. He would buy his mother a big house, much like the one he would have in California. He would send his family money and vitamins, and they would be the envy of all the relatives. He would take up golf and drink single-malt scotch, learn to speak English, and make new friends. On Christmas cards, he would sit between Melanie and Vivian, his arms around both of them. Sometimes a stranger, usually a woman, would ask if Melanie was his younger sister, and if his mother-in-law wasn't around, Xiao Gang would lean in with a smile and say, "Yes."

LOVE

Fuerdai to the Max

IT IS TECHNICALLY an unhappy occasion, but I am crazy happy to see Kenny. I spot him in the crowd right away, all the way from the sidewalk of the airport. My dad's driver, Six Uncle, who is obligated to follow me everywhere now, says, "Look at that little filthy bastard," loud enough for me to hear and slams down on the horn with a balled-up fist.

Kenny's a lot skinnier than he was the last time I saw him; his hair isn't gelled anymore and it flops around the top of his head like a fin. For the first time, I think I might be bigger than he is. His expression is grim until he spots me and sticks his tongue out.

As Kenny pushes through the crowded sidewalk, I catch a nearby couple turning around and giving him dirty looks. Maybe they can tell from the brand of his suitcase or the smell of his cologne, but there must also be something distinct and

77

intangible; I know it because I have it, too. Some people think being called a *fuerdai*—second-generation rich—is an insult, but I don't care. The emphasis is on the *fu,* as in rich. And Kenny and I, we are *fuerdai* to the max.

Twice a year we come home to Beijing to visit our families. Usually, no matter how busy they are, our parents pick us up from the airport and together we go to town on spicy seafood at our favorite place on Ghost Street. This year we're on our own. Our parents have their reasons to be pissed off. Kenny and I are both back because we have done something really bad. It isn't even a visit anymore, since neither of us can go back to the States anytime soon.

When we were fifteen, our parents took us to Cerritos, the city they were told had the top high school in SoCal, so we could enjoy a full-on American education. Complete with American suburban life. Most of us were wards of the same Chinese lawyer couple, the ones who promised to get us into college. Our parents bought Kenny and me matching cars, laptops, and clothes, and then, even though I practically begged my mom to stay the year, left us there. The lawyer couple said we'd get used to American life right away. We had neighboring two-bedroom condos in the same complex, and a lady who never talked to us came around once a week to clean up, wash our clothes, and buy our groceries.

None of the white kids, the Mexicans, the Koreans, and the ABCs, even the ones who spoke Chinese well, wanted anything much to do with us. In class they called me Skinny Chinese Sam because there was already another Chinese Sam and he was fat. Kenny was always our leader. Kenny was Kenny because he liked *South Park* and everyone thought he was funny. He had a way about him that made everyone stick around. Our core group consisted of the two Sams, Kenny, a crazy girl named Lily who kept us all on short leashes, and, of course, that idiot who named himself Cloud.

"Goddamn, I need a smoke so bad right now," says Kenny as he throws his suitcase in the backseat of the car.

"Six Uncle, can you give him a cigarette?" I ask.

Dad's driver pulls a soft pack out of his breast pocket and tosses it in Kenny's direction without looking at us, then gets back in the front. He's been with my dad since I was two years old; I can't even count how many times he's had to lie for me. So only he can get away with treating me and my friends like that.

"How bad was it back there?" I ask Kenny, reaching the flame of the lighter toward him. We both lean back against the car window as he takes his first satisfied inhale.

"Don't want to talk about it. Too much on my mind," Kenny says, exhaling like a dragon through his nose. "I couldn't pack my own bags. Had to leave all my stuff and run out of the house before dawn like a thief or something."

"Shit, that sucks, and you just got the Huracán, too!"

"Let's not talk about it. I'm so fucking sick of talking about it," he says, spitting on the sidewalk and wiping it away with his Nikes.

I nod my head. Fair enough.

"My mom knows you're here to get me, right?" he asks quietly.

"Yeah, but she told my mom to tell me to tell you that she doesn't want to see you yet."

"That's good," he says, "because I don't want to see her either."

"Well, I'm glad you're back, bro," I say, and I genuinely mean it. He flicks his cigarette over the car and we both get in the back. Six Uncle stares at me in the mirror and then shakes his head. I turn the stereo up with my iPhone, so loud that the sunroof shakes.

This was actually maybe only the first time in my life that I've ever truly messed up. I didn't lose money in Vegas, I didn't drag race, and I didn't have that many friends to rage with on the weekends. I took molly a few times at some EDM parties in Orange County, but who hasn't? I did once get myself in trouble with the cops. All I was doing was cruising, trying to come down. I was this close to making it home but must have fallen asleep and nearly wiped out on the mountain road. Instead of driving off the cliff, I smeared blue paint all along the retaining wall and had to ditch my car there. I figured one day I'd tell my kids, "See that? Your pops drew that."

Took me about an hour to walk home and I passed out on my bed immediately, but later, when police were inside my condo and couldn't find any parents, it became just a giant mess. I called the Chinese lawyer couple, who showed up and jabbed their fingers in my face, and called up a white-man lawyer. They said because I was over eighteen, there was a chance I'd be convicted of reckless driving and then get locked up. After that, the lawyers told my parents that it would be better to have me back in Beijing, at least for a while.

I heard my dad talking to the lawyers on the phone, saying how much he'd be willing to pay them as a reward to cover this up. I think the more trouble I get into, the bigger my dad gets to feel for getting me out of it.

That's the only reason I already had a flight to Beijing scheduled for the morning after "the incident." By the time the police tried to find me at school, I was out of the country. They couldn't keep our names straight anyway. Zhang, Ming, Yuyao, Jirui, Kao, Duo Duo, Fung, it was all the same to the cops. They couldn't tell us apart, they didn't know if a person was missing, just thought it was one person with three names or three people with the same name. So even though I was there that night, nobody will see my name in any newspapers or getting bad press for Chinese parachute kids. Nothing about my parents, about the one-child policy, about Chinese society failing my generation. My parents didn't even seem that mad at me about any of it. It was not as if I was throwing away a bright future at Berkeley that was all lined up, they'd probably given up on that dream a long time ago.

What police reports can't say were our reasons for doing what we did. California high schools can be treacherous places. Think about it: What would you do if, on the first day of school, assholes keyed your new car because they thought you wouldn't fight back? Wouldn't you want everyone to know that you could defend yourself? Wouldn't you want revenge? Wouldn't you want people to understand that if anyone messed with your friends or your family, then you would make them pay?

Before that night, I might have done a few other things that were against the law. I may or may not have punched a kid so hard in middle school that he had to wear a brace. I admit to taking some bats to car doors after being looked at wrong. You could say I baited trouble. But the thing is, I always did what I wanted and nothing happened to me. Just good luck. What Lily asked me to do, what she convinced me was necessary, well, that was just bad luck. Especially for her, for Kenny and Fat Sam, too, but more so for fucking Cloud.

Instead of taking us straight back to my parents' place, I convince Six Uncle to let us eat first at an Italian supermarket in Shin Kong Place, where they have really good spaghetti.

Six Uncle watches us order, then pays for our food, but as soon as he heads to the bathroom Kenny and I drop our forks and get the hell out of there. We run out the back way through the hanging hams and into the mall. It is always like that with us. We could speak without even talking. We're both hysterical and panting and pulling up our pants and Kenny is leading the way, hurtling down the escalator yelling, "Emergency, ladies and gentlemen! A life is on the line!"

Now that's the Kenny I missed. In Beijing, Kenny was a legend. Kenny always had, like, six girlfriends and a limp, which he claims he got from fucking too much. He has always been lanky even though he eats like a beast. And although he was practically military royalty, he never held that over anyone's head. He was always chill, fun to be around, and even though he had lots of friends, he always called me up. Being around him actually calms me down a lot; he is probably the closest thing I have to a brother.

Once outside, we jump in a black cab in the alley and head back up the second ring road toward Sanlitun.

"Can you take us to Kokomo?" asks Kenny. Kokomo is a cheesy tiki bar on the roof of 3.3 Mall, where nobody would know us. "I could use some sunshine right now."

I turn my phone over in my hand and take out the battery. Kenny never got his phone back after being released from the police station, but his credit cards still work, which is a relief.

"I should get hammered before I see my parents," he mumbles, as if to himself. He is looking ahead, but his eyes are all spacey. The hand with his wallet in it seems to be shaking.

It is depressing just to look at him.

"Stop being so worried," I say in the most convincing tone I can come up with. "They've heard of far worse. Kids in pool-hall shootings, killing people. I heard my dad tell your dad, 'It's not like he killed anyone.'"

I look into the rearview mirror just in time to see the driver turn his eyes away.

"My dad's not like yours."

"Yeah, you're right," I say. "Maybe my dad is just tired of getting mad. He's tired of me in general."

"I think my dad is literally going to kill himself," Kenny says, not looking at me.

"Just stick with the story. Keep saying 'It was all Cloud, that's the guy you want to question,'" I say. "People will forget about it eventually." But Kenny's not listening.

Kenny laughs. "You know if this gets out, that his son got

into big trouble in the States, what are people going to say? They're going to want to know where all my money came from."

I shake my head like that's ridiculous, but what do I know?

The counterfeit liquor at Kokomo tastes like gasoline and the music is terrible techno, so it is exactly where nobody will come looking for us. Kenny's scared and so am I. His nervous energy rushes through me like a wild fire looking for the next spot to burn.

We need to order a ton of beers, we yell to the waitress.

As it gets dark above us, we crowd the table with empty bottles. Kenny loosens up. He tells me about being handcuffed and driven to the police station. He tells me about not showering for four days and finding out he is actually capable of BO. He tells me about not being able to take a shit for three days and pissing in a bucket. He tells me about using his one phone call to call his "aunt" and finding out she was more scared than he was. He tells me about the rotten milk the guards threw at him and the peanut butter sandwiches he couldn't swallow. Even then, the way he tells it, it's pretty funny. The way he talks makes me think he doesn't hate me, won't blame me for what happened, at least not right now. He tells me about making bail and finding his real aunt from Florida waiting to pick him up.

"She was standing outside the police station wearing a disguise, like an actual wig and sunglasses, like she's conducting espionage in a movie," he says. I spit my beer out all over the table, laughing.

We try to remember the numbers of everyone we like in

the city, but we've been away for a long time. Plus it isn't summer vacation and nobody studying abroad would be around yet. Our friend Square is still in the international school here, and after a while he comes by, even though he never liked me and always made sure I could tell. Then Coco and Crystal arrive, these annoying girls we know from elementary school who are no fun and just shop all day.

"Kenny? Hey, Kenny. I was just thinking about you," says Crystal as soon as she sees us.

They kiss Kenny on both cheeks. They don't do it to me, but I keep my face straight.

"Yeah, what were you thinking about?" asks Kenny.

"I was thinking that, well, I haven't texted Kenny in a while, and I wondered how you were doing."

"I'm—" he starts to say, but Crystal isn't finished talking.

"Coco just went to Moscow with her mom because she had this idea in her mind that she wanted to buy diamonds," she continues. "But of course it was a big waste of time. Then I just got back from London because I. M. Pei built my dad's friend a pavilion in his backyard, but that party was boring, too. What do you guys do over there?"

"Nothing special, just going to school. Going to Six Flags. Car shows. Pretty girls. Smoking leaves," he says.

"And how about you?" I cut in. "How's school in Switzerland?"

"No, Sweden," she replies shortly. "We drive to Norway and listen to these bands in the woods and eat seafood."

"Right, right, Sweden," Kenny says, nodding, as if agreeing to something dangerous.

"Well, Kenny and I, we've been well. I keep telling Kenny

that we should come back more often," I say. "Just to keep up with you sophisticated European girls."

"So tell me," Crystal asks, "what's it like in America, is it all that great?"

"Yeah, sure," I say, looking away from her and making eye contact with the girls at the next table. "It's pretty weird."

We jump around the dance floor in a group just like the old junior high times. More friends of Coco and Crystal show up. Someone carrying a briefcase pays for a private room and like magic, the top-notch local girls line up at the railing, trying not to look in our direction, hoping we will invite them inside.

"It's still fun, right?" I say to Kenny, eyeing the girls. "Don't you kind of miss this?"

"Why aren't they asking us why we're back so early? Do they know something? Did you tell them?" Kenny asks, jerking his head toward Coco and Crystal.

"Man, nobody knows anything. They don't care," I whisper, patting him on the back.

Coco is busy lecturing the waiter, "Champagne has to come from Champagne. This shit is just sparkling wine." And the friends she brought are nodding even though they don't care and the waiter is listening even though I'm sure he cares even less. They're all flirting with this tall, muscly guy who is not paying for anything because he's someone's private tutor. He apparently went to Harvard, Yale, and Princeton, and yet he is mooching off us.

Then Kenny says he wants to "fly," so we have to ask around for Prince's new number. Prince is a collective of Nigerian drug dealers who refers to themselves as Prince. Whether this is a sophisticated operation or Prince is actually a real person is a debate no one really wants to engage in.

"Do you want the green or do you want the white or do you want the black?" Prince says to me in English.

"The green," I yell into the phone, still loving the way my American accent sounds. We go into the bathroom together to smoke the weed and I close the door to shut out the sounds of our friends singing karaoke.

"You feel better now?" I say to Kenny as he tries to light the joint in his mouth. "It's going to be fine."

I turn on the fan and watch him inhale as much smoke as he possibly can.

"Feel better . . . that we fucked up our entire lives?" he says in between huge hits.

I think I am looking at him way too much, so I look away when he catches my eye.

"What would you rather have happened? For us to just walk away?" I say, taking the joint from him. "Was it wrong of me to try to help Lily? To stand up for one of us?"

"Oh, so that was why you made us do it," Kenny says, lean- his face on the mirror. "Thanks for that. I feel great now ing up my life. Probably my whole family's lives, too."

a joke? Was Kenny crying or laughing?

u were there, too. You could have stopped it if you ay, but he's so high I'm not sure he hears me.

alked up to this bitch named Wey in the her baby-blue Maserati. We told her to come with us to the park by the condos, we had to talk to her. I remember that part clearly: the two kids playing with that big white dog tied outside the ice cream place. Those orange-and-white clouds hurrying across the sky above our heads as we walked. Green ivy smell in the breeze. There was only one tree in the park and we gathered under its branches. I told Wey to admit she was wrong and apologize to Lily, but she gave me two miles of lip. Then I told her to beg Lily for forgiveness, but she just kept talking shit.

In her gravelly smoker's voice, this bitch said that Lily was not who she said she was. Said Lily was an escort. That her family doesn't do arms deals and they don't really have that much money and that's why she keeps the Four Seasons room because they were whoring her out. That we were stupid to be her friends, that she was using us. Wey said we were trash, too, because we went to public school. Then she started yelling, saying we were all in big trouble now for trying to intimidate her, that her family was politically connected, like that was going to scare us. The only person she scared was Cloud, who kept telling me to calm down. I told him to shut up or scram. But Cloud ended up standing by the edge of the park, waiting, maybe because he was looking out for other cars or because he was scared or didn't have a ride. The rest of us, we were a children of Somebody. Maybe not tippy top of the food cha but still she had the nerve to look down on us and our fami Who would we be if we just let that go?

Lily pushed the bitch first and started slapping her ar I said, "Make her kneel and kiss our shoes." Then F told her to clean up the cigarette butts off the ground mouth. Then Lily dumped her milk tea on Wey's head it," Lily said while recording with her phone. "You're a psycho and a liar. We won't let you go until you admit it."

What did Wey think was going to happen? That we would just let her get away with saying whatever she wanted?

I still remember the way that bitch looked when I grabbed her by the hair and told her to take her clothes off. Her flat ass all white as she bent over, trying to hide her floppy boobs with her knees. I laughed in her face. And then everybody started cracking up. By then she was crying, but it was too late for that. Her ugly face was smudged like a clown's. I remember Lily spitting on her and me burning her with the end of my cigarette before Kenny pulled me off. After that we were all quiet. The mood changed quickly. Walking back to our cars across the big intersection, none of us looked at one another.

Maybe Kenny thought I'd taken it too far, but I felt pretty numb while it was happening. Why should I care? Nobody cared what I did. I never had anybody to answer to. I watched my friends speed off in their cars. I remember being the last to leave. It was hard to turn the car on because my hands kept shaking.

It is still early, so I tell the server to bring some fruit platters and another bottle and to welcome some pretty girls in.

I wake up in Square's apartment. I know this because I recognize the paintings of brown rocks on the walls, which Square was telling us cost a million dollars each. Also because his mom is yelling my name.

"Minnie is on the phone and Six Uncle is coming to get you," she says with a sigh.

I give her a thumbs-up.

My parents needed me to give them English names, so I gave them a list and they managed to pick Donald and Minnie, just like the Disney characters. It makes them easier for foreign partners to remember and for Chinese clients to bypass Confucian hierarchy.

Square's housemaid leaves a bowl of congee on the coffee table and I sit there staring at it. I would be scared if Donald was on the line. I could see him having to leave his study, not having finished pouring hot water over his collection of clay teapots as if they were living things. My dad has had nothing handed to him. My grandma died when he was just a kid, but he never talks about it. In graduate school he managed to study for a year in Bologna, which is where he picked up Italian, but he didn't tell me about that either. It was my mom who told me that Dad was once so poor he ate cheap canned meat with rice for months until another student pointed out that it was cat food. How does one go from eating cat food to making himself a millionaire? He doesn't tell me when I ask. My dad never really let me get to know him. It's like he thinks he already pays for my life, so what else do I expect from him? To open up to me? I am just something he puts up with because I'm his son.

Donald used to make me porridge with the cans of sardines he always took with him on trips. He would pour on soy sauce and smash into it whatever was left in the fridge and then at the last minute he'd pour in some hot water and call it the emperor's porridge. Minnie thought it was disgusting and would open the windows. But when I think about it, I only remember how good it had tasted.

Then when I got older, he'd order takeout, always the most

expensive dishes at whatever restaurant he happened to be eating at with his friends. He always got two orders. "Because my son is a big boy." Six Uncle usually drove the food back to me fresh. Abalone steak, racks of ribs, and once a dozen live prawns still convulsing in their rice wine bath. Donald uses me to brag to his friends about how complete his life is. The way he uses Mom to show off her closet full of purses right by our front door.

My mom feels like my sister sometimes because I always remember her looking so young and fragile. In elementary school, I cursed at teachers just to get in trouble, just to see my mom's worried face outside the classroom window, coming to get me. When I got kicked out of my first school, she sent me to live with her mom and never came to visit me. That was when I felt like no matter how much I acted up, nobody cared about me anymore. I could do whatever I wanted. These days what I'm most afraid of is Mom being nice to me.

I look for Kenny, but he's not in the living room and I don't see his shoes by the door. Maybe he was right to be afraid for his dad. He was a pretty prominent public figure in the municipal government. If all the details got out, I could see it being a pretty big scandal. But as long as Kenny just sticks to the story I told him before, it would be okay. It was all Cloud. We were just watching. We couldn't stop him from doing what he did.

The problem with Los Angeles was that there's no weather and too much space. I needed the weight of a city to distract me. In the suburbs there was nothing going on, so I started focusing on the people around me, and I inevitably found somebody I couldn't stand.

It was common knowledge that Cloud's dad had been in jail for corruption since Cloud was a kid. We all knew his dad used to be Lily's dad's right-hand man. Basically that meant Cloud's education was compensation, a kind of reward for the job well done of his dad's keeping his mouth shut. We all knew this because none of our parents would stop talking about it. What a good student Cloud was. How humble. How big and strong. How respectful he was to his minders. How he was the only one making the most of every opportunity in America.

Cloud's looks didn't do him any favors either.

When he smiled, his gums showed above his teeth, like a dog's. His head was shaped like a Buddha statue's and he had an effeminate way of talking with his hands, so much that I was always noticing how clean his nails were. When we were having a good time picking out new cars, he inevitably said something to dampen the mood: "Guys, I calculated the cost of insurance for internationals. Those companies are ripping us off. You should really just explore different modes of public transportation."

When we were all talking about majoring in business in college, he said, "I am thinking of engineering. Because I think with engineering you really have a chance in this country. There's the infrastructure for all talented parties to succeed."

"Oh god, shut up already," I would say, but then Kenny kept stopping me. "No, don't tell him to shut up, I want to know. One day we're going to be visiting our boy Cloud at Harvard."

When waitresses put cans of tea with straws in front of us, Cloud never took one unless I offered, because I always paid. I didn't like the idea of visiting Cloud at Harvard.

Had the circumstances been different, I wouldn't have had

any reason to talk to him. Half the time, I was embarrassed to be seen with such a dork in public.

"They probably only need one person to place the blame on," I said to Kenny over the phone right afterward. "The white cops looking at photos won't know the difference between you and Cloud. I promise you that."

If Kenny said Cloud was the leader, I honestly thought the police would believe it since he is the biggest and tallest of all of us. When they figured out he was already accepted to Johns Hopkins early admission and, more important, a total wimp, they'd assume it was a big mistake and let everyone off the hook. It had seemed like a good idea since Cloud was the only one without the money to run back to China, and for whatever deal he had going on with Lily's dad, he would never rat her out.

So it was a huge surprise to me when they didn't let Cloud go and more shocking when they came to school and pulled Kenny, Lily, and Fat Sam out of class and took them into the station for questioning. Nobody was prepared for it to get so official. How were we supposed to know that the bitch would actually press charges?

Kenny was lucky to have gotten out of the country before he officially got charged. None of the Chinese newspapers had picked up anything about it yet. I didn't want to agree with Kenny, but this could turn out really bad for his dad if—well, I could see the headlines. If somebody really decides to push for it, I could see how Kenny's dad might get flagged for corruption and it would be Kenny's fault.

To be honest, if I were in Kenny's place and I had my family's reputation to protect, maybe I'd just kill myself.

I know where to do it, too. I've given it some thought. There's one stretch of the PCH where there isn't a single traffic light for miles. Every time I drive past, there are always flowers clustered against a pole and right where the road bends. If you were to crash there, nobody would think anything of it.

Lily somehow found out about my reckless driving case and never told a single person about it. In fact, she said I was lucky to get to start over and there was no point in making it public. That was the kind of thing that got me thinking I liked Lily. She was completely her own creation and never lost her calm, so you could count on her to step up for you. I respected that about her. A girl like Lily, with everything she had, isn't allowed to be soft. She can't just cry over a breeze.

So when she told me about that bitch named Wey trolling her online, spreading rumors about her and so-and-so's boyfriend from Vancouver, I didn't care about any of the details because she cried softly as she was telling me. It made me want to grab her face and kiss her. One summer almost a year ago, Lily invited me to visit her hotel room at the Four Seasons. It was just a room with a big bed and all these Christmas decorations still hanging off the wall. There was one of those enormous teddy bears from Costco on a pile of sheepskin rugs and half-empty bottles of water rolling around on the floor. There was nothing else to drink, which is why I think nothing ended up happening between us. Maybe people think I am very experienced with girls, but I don't really know how to talk to them. Like if I get really wasted, sometimes I end up in bed with a girl without me having to say anything, but I don't really know how to take it there if we're both sober. I think my feelings for Lily started that night because I saw something in her that none of the rest of them saw. That she was just as lost as me and even more alone. It was then that I vowed to myself that I'd do anything for her. But she didn't have the same feelings for me, because she just saw what everyone else saw, that I could be mean and I liked fighting. There was really nothing I could do about that.

I wait until Square's mom leaves before I go looking for my shoes. When I find them I stuff my feet in without untying them. I know the servants' entrance to Square's building, so I ditch the congee bowl on a table and escape down the stairs and into the hutong entrance behind the apartment complex. I just want to go as far away as I can, but it's just then I remember I still don't have any money. My hand hurts and I stick it into my mouth. It tastes like blood and I realize there are nasty cuts on each of my knuckles. I vaguely remember Kenny and me yelling at each other, me throwing a few punches at him that land on a glass wall. I wonder what's wrong with me, what makes me keep going further and further into fucking up my relationships with people until they give up on me.

"Young man, that's going to get infected if you keep doing that."

I turn around and see an old man with a shaved head and a tank top sitting on a stool watching me. The words TEAR DOWN are painted in red script above his head.

"Come in my house and I'll give you something to wash it off with," he says.

I think it's probably better to stay off the street in case Six Uncle is looking for me, so I follow him into the shade.

It is the garbage collector's house. By house I mean it's just a room filled with trash. There must be at least ten broken fans in this place. There are three women of different ages watching a small television, and they ignore me. Pieces of cloth cover a moldy cement wall. There's a baby, so tiny it couldn't have been a year old, sleeping facedown on a bottom bunk. The baby's butt is dirty, and it's lying on an even dirtier bamboo mat. There are long ribbons attached to the ceiling fan, perhaps to keep the flies and mosquitoes flying in circles.

The old man hands me a pail of fresh water and I dip my hand in it. The coolness stings but feels good. He gives me a wedge of iodine-soaked bandage and I thank him even though it hurts to use it.

Then the little baby wakes up and starts crying at the top of its lungs. It's like a signal for the whole family to get ready for some big event. The whole house is in action. I guess it is the mom who ducks out of the room and comes back. She is holding a piece of glass, almost the size of an egg, suspended on a string. It looks like a broken-off strand of crystal from a chandelier. She holds the baby and gently swings the glass above her head. Between the television light, the sunlight, and the lights on in the house, the glass throws a thousand colors around us and, like magic, the baby stops crying.

I have to admit, if only for that fleeting moment, I feel something, too.

Home Remedies for
Non–Life-Threatening Ailments

Boredom (Born from general confusion stemming from lack of clear direction/complete misunderstanding of life's purpose.)

Stay indoors, in a room with bad lighting but many makeshift ashtrays. Arrange and rearrange your comforter into various malleable structures. Stand back and give names to the newly birthed forms. Now it is a manatee. Now it is Abraham Lincoln's headless body. Now it is a giant nose. Applaud yourself for your mastery, for now you can be fairly certain of the potential you possess as a visual artist.

Write a letter to the boy named Bunny whom you met on a train in Croatia. The one who spoke to trees and set his watch to random hours as his way of time traveling; write to him that you hope he is still alive and insane. Tell him you are glad you're not him and even more glad he's no longer following you around, talking about modernism.

Grief (Not your own grief, but your father's grief, after your fourteen-year-old dog dies. He calls often, sobbing into the receiver. Even though he's a fifty-five-year-old man who should know that a blind asthmatic basset hound was not going to live forever. Grief that hardens when you realize that life has gradually become very difficult for your father, and you're at a loss as to how to comfort him. There are many ways of living, places to hang hopes and direct love, and it's quite obvious to you that a very old dog was probably not a good place to hang his. So it's specifically that kind of grief.)

Let his phone calls ring and ring. Delete voice messages robotically, holding the phone away from your ear. If your heart is the fruit from which the nectar of comforting words could be squeezed, that fruit is dry. The dregs could be called mockery. They would sting him bitterly.

It is better to focus on a problem you can help him solve. How about those giant squirrels that have taken over his backyard? Eating the grass bald in patches, like alien spaceship landings. Order poison that he couldn't use when he had a dog around. When all the squirrels are dead, the guilt that both of you will share is sure to keep him from calling you for at least two weeks.

Inappropriate Feelings (Toward married contemporary British drama professors.)

Go to his office hours religiously, bringing in new opinions on plays he'd recommended. Show him the plays you've written inspired by the plays he's asked you to read. Fiddle with the framed photos on his desk as you talk about your family, his hometown, your boyfriend, and his wife. Laugh a lot. Babysit his three-year-old daughter, Elaine, and while she's asleep, go to his room and smell his shirts.

Agree to go to dinner with him downtown, tell him things about your father you've never told anyone else. You will begin to feel queasy when you realize this is the first time you've ever been alone with him outside of school. When he asks you up to his studio loft to show you his sculptures, say "Cool! Definitely!" with eyebrows arched. When he goes to stroke your hair, act surprised, say something antiquated like "Oh my!"

Take his clothes off while making out with him on his couch. Make mental notes of the peculiarity of his needy old-man lips, his loose old-man skin, and his strange rubbery old-man hard-on. Something will happen right then that'll make him seem less a sexy, gentle intellectual and more just like the guy who "hey hey heys" at you outside the bodega. Your inappropriate feelings will then be dissolved into a satisfied curiosity and now you can pull back, walk out of the apartment, and leave him naked, bewildered, gasping.

Self-Doubt (In your abilities as a playwright stemming from Inappropriate Feelings toward married contemporary British drama professors.)

Switch your major to archaeology, to criminology, to library science. Take a semester off to work at a florist across town that specializes in enormous bouquets and fountains.

Write a play about a large, wrinkly alien who terrorizes Los Angeles.

Fear of Flying (Because every time you fly, you land somewhere new and you have to make new friends.)

Leave something you love in every city you've lived in. A record player in Shanghai, a kitten in Seattle, your best dresses hanging in a closet in Paris. That way you'll always have a reason to retrace your steps back to old friends. So it means you won't have to stay away forever. Learn to enjoy being alone, appreciate the silence of dinners where an entire roast duck can be gnawed away, cartilage and all, without conversational interruption. You are free and oh-so-mysterious. Think: Friends, who needs friends?

Bilingual Heartache (From someone breaking your heart in a foreign language. It is like regular heartache but somehow it's painful in a creative, new way.)

Pray that a painful cold sore appears on your face so that you can instead wallow in self-pity.

Self-Pity (A by-product of chronic dissatisfaction with your wide, uninteresting face.)

Get your nails done by a seventeen-year-old Vietnamese girl who probably weighs about as much as one of your thighs. After she puts your hands in a bowl of smelly water, she rubs lotion into your fingers. She looks up at your face and says, "Your hands are so white and soft, you never do any housework, do you?"

Open your mouth to protest, as if she were your mother, but then agree; she guessed correctly. Nod. Lower your head.

Dwelling on the Past (You remember seeing your parents waltzing in the living room of the first house you lived in. You think about your father on his knees like a wounded animal, bent over the newspaper looking for work. You hear the echoes of your mother sobbing in the shower on your way to elementary school. These memories become a fable, entitled "The Legend of Mom and Dad," and it is tied to you like a cloud-shaped balloon above your head.)

Begin researching random things of interest. The history of Jamaica, for example, and the tragic disappearance of indigenous people is a good place to start. Start a blog about Jamaica and Jamaican cuisine. Establish a huge Internet presence.

Insomnia (Because now that you spend so much time on the Internet in order to avoid Dwelling on the Past.)

Make paper planes with *New Yorker* subscription postcards. Rearrange bedroom furniture. Tipple Nyquil from the bottle, and as your arms go numb and your chest sinks to the bottom of the mattress, think how much better life is now. Really! Your parents are no longer married, but everyone is eating high-quality local organic produce, only they're eating it alone and now no one gets to argue. Isn't that better?

Desperation (General lustiness with no valid prospects.)

Make up a long sordid story about the time you made out with a bartender who looked exactly like Joseph Gordon-Levitt (could it have been another Gordon-Levitt brother?) and then proceeded to fuck him on a park bench. You were wearing black leather boots up to your thighs like Catwoman, and you straddled him right there, under the moonlight, in front of that bagel shop you like. People could have been making bagels for the following day and they could have watched you. You know what? They were and they did. You are a woman of incredible sexual prowess, you are wild, and you are trouble.

Tell this story to your friends, their friends, even your brother. Watch their faces as you imitate Gordon-Levitt's O face.

Double Shame (The first shame is when your grandmother, with her crooked stroke-ruined face, shits herself when you have friends over. The smell of shit fills the house, your friends file out, and you are filled with shame. Now comes the second shame, in that you realize you love your grandmother and without her there is no you. She has survived so much with bravery and dignity. How could you think these things about her? More shame. Double-edged shame. Double double shame.)

Kiss her on the cheek until she loves you again. Until you make-believe she forgives you. Until you make-believe you forgive yourself. You try to avoid her on weekends. You stop inviting friends over. Every time you are filled with this double shame, you smother her wrinkly cheek with kisses.

Regrets (Big ones. They look just like your mother's and they are getting worse. On top of inheriting her big laugh, you also got these: her regrets. Not wanting to disappoint others, leading to betrayal of self, romantic failures, and loss of hope. Marrying the wrong man leads to a lifetime of unhappiness. Her regrets overtake you, until you drink her bitterness and cry her tears. These big regrets your mother gave to you, they take root, scratch, and grow.)

Take on the persona of a really matter-of-fact, optimistic young lady. Occasionally spout aphorisms like "I believe in happy endings!" and "It'll all work out for the better!" You hope this will soothe her regrets before they somehow permanently become yours.

It's worth a shot. After all, your mother is still your closest friend and you are afraid to ever be without her.

Family Pressure (Not directed at you, but at your much-older brother's marriage issue. His hair is receding, they say. You must act fast! It is your responsibility! How can you go on with your own life knowing that he, your very own brother, has no wife and child! How can he live like this! So lonely like this?)

Promise your parents and grandparents that you will find your much-older brother a suitable wife. Say you'll introduce him to your older friends, your language tutor, and there's even the neighbor of a friend whose party you went to who is probably single.

Don't actually do anything. Why would you do something?

Humiliation (From listening to the guy you're sleeping with chatting to his out-of-town girlfriend on the phone, in your bathroom.)

Act really cavalier about his having a girlfriend. You are not like other girls, you say, and demonstrate it by bringing up how "cool" with everything you really are. Watch his director's reel while wearing his socks. He holds your hands when you sleep and you wake up smiling. This is love, you think.

Imagine throwing yourself against him, an imaginary camera following at half speed, as lights blur and you're suddenly more darling than you really are. And he will turn around and see you with this fine-boned teary face and realize it's you he's loved all along. It could all be different, you tell yourself, if only.

After that, stop seeing him and start dating a tax lawyer named Linus. Linus barely has time for one girlfriend.

Terrible Taste (In boyfriends, marked by erratic, impulsive decisions based on purely subjective and questionably assigned qualities. One bad choice after another. Each worse in previously unexplored categories. A long time ago a boy said that you purred like a cat while you were asleep. The tax lawyer finally says, "You know you fucking snore, right?" He also says your feet are fat.)

Look down at your feet. Your stupid little feet and your sausage toes.

Confusion (While visiting your much-older brother's newly purchased well-furnished condo, find a DVD collection entitled *Sexiest Gay Romp, Miami!* Maybe it was mislabeled? Stare at the framed pictures of his first and only girlfriend, study her dull eyes. Maybe she's just really nice? Remember all the times he flirted obnoxiously with waitresses, does that mean anything? Think of his devotion to church, the time he took you to an NSYNC concert, does that mean anything?)

Tell your family your brother has impossible standards and you don't bring up the DVDs with him. There are some things you cannot say to your older brother. He keeps you at arm's length, as if you've never grown out of being a nosy toddler. Mysteriously you still love him, but you don't know if he knows. You keep his secret and you don't try to comfort him. Does this mean anything?

Wanton Tenderness (Mercenary empathy for strangers you have nothing to do with.)

When the old man alone in the restaurant begs someone

on the phone to join him for dinner, resist the urge to comfort him. Watch him order all the dishes again once the first round gets cold and fight the inclination to join his sadness.

Seriously consider adopting a slightly disabled cat.

Baby Fever (Contracted while Instagram-stalking your neighbors who are not only good-looking but seem in love and full of hope. You've never wanted a baby, but now you're cooing and making faces at all of them.)

Realize that the last thing you want to do is procreate with the man-child tax lawyer. His hair is receding so far up his head it's almost as if he has space for an extra face. His eyes don't look kind; what would your children look like? Break up with yet another boyfriend.

Stomachaches (Having ignored his phone calls, your father now comes over to your apartment bearing cream puffs. You are initially happy. You love cream puffs! But then he, once again, tells you his divorce story. How your mother cruelly told him she never loved him and how lonely he's been his entire adult life. He describes to you his past mistresses, girls your age, who also never loved him. He is losing his shit, he is crying. You stuff your mouth with cream puffs so you can't say anything. You eat an obscene amount of cream puffs. You swallow without chewing so you don't set off another round of tears. But now you have a stomachache.)

Move to a city a thousand miles away.

Longing (After you realized that every real lover you've ever had has moved on and perhaps you haven't got a clue about what you're doing. Longing that tastes bitter like your fingers after you absentmindedly kiss them while remembering someone else doing the same.)

Make friends with women in their forties and let them give you long lectures about freezing your eggs.

Take everything beautiful in every relationship you've ever had and bring it down to a word. "Fedora." "Champagne." "Objectification." "Fetish."

Cry.

Anxiety (Stemming from unfulfilled potential, general nail-biting about the future.)

Stop drinking coffee, start rolling cigarettes, bake cookies and share.

Gain weight and fret.

Fag Hag Fever (Puking outside of a gay club after too many tequila shots while your gay best friend rubs your now whale-size back mechanically, as if he were washing a minivan. In your drunken rampage, you ask him if you two were the last people on earth, would he consider a domestic partnership?)

Join a gym and torture yourself. Once you become skinny again, you can puke outside of regular clubs.

Discomfort (From seeing your mother kissing another man.)

Stare at the bouquet of white lilies on the kitchen island with disdain; will them to die with your hatred.

Sadness (Visiting your father in his big house alone, surrounded by plasma televisions, a fridge full of beer, and a computer full of porn, and he asks you to play another round of Wii with him.)

Take him shopping for new clothes, sign him up for dating websites, and discuss the women with whom he chats on the

Internet. Act as if it's not incredibly disturbing to you, though it is. When he calls you, slurring his words, on a Saturday night, drive to whatever bar he's at. Collect his things, carry him to his car, take him home, tuck him in, and never mention it to him because he will not remember.

Sadness (Gay brother sadness.)

Suggest a weekend trip to San Francisco, where the two of you go to museums, line up for brunch, and taste wine in Napa. He gives you many good side hugs and laughs at all your stories. As the BART train is about to pull into the station, agree that you've both had a marvelous time. As the train arrives, your long hair flies up like a curtain around your face and only when the wheels have reached their crescendo shout to him, "Treat me as an equal! Be open and honest with me!" "What did you say?" he shouts back. When the train's doors open, you reply, "Nothing."

Sadness (General sadness about the futility of life.)

Drink.

Sadness (For your mother never having been in love.)

Pick a night when your mother's running errands. Sneak in, break the water pipes, and flood the house. Three inches of water will cover the living room; the carpet will be a beige sponge. The wood floors your dad put in himself years ago will flare out at the edges like books turned upside down.

When your mother opens the door, water will pour over her feet into the garage. She will turn on the light and then turn it off, afraid of the electric shock. In the dark your mother will scoop water out of the house with bowls and buckets. She will unplug appliances dutifully.

She will call you, excited and giddy. Her sad disposition will be broken with the thrill. She will be laughing and splashing when she tells you something exciting has happened. A big undeniable something!

Vaulting the Sea

BY THE TIME they were teenagers, Taoyu knew every muscle in his partner's back. As their bodies ascended the parallel steps to the diving board, he could trace from memory the particular slope of Hai's shoulder blades. He knew, like the veins on a leaf, the path that the water would travel, from his thighs to the rungs below his feet.

At the top, he counted out loud: three, two . . .

In the air, they were one body reflected in a mirror. A dancer in a glittering spectacle whose pirouettes begin and end as quickly as a flash of lightning. Always the stronger diver must compensate for the weaker one, and without having to make eye contact, Taoyu knew where Hai was in the air at all times. He knew Hai's eyelashes would touch his knees on the first revolution and then his warm breath would burst out in front of him at the extension. To the people in the stands, they looked like two wings of a single bird. The pool was the sea and the impact an embrace.

Nothing else existed from the moment Taoyu reached the edge of the board to the moment he ripped into the water. The water burst open in a cosmic flower, blooming exuberantly before disappearing, its fizzing petals melting back into stillness.

In those seconds, Taoyu denied all sense of himself until he felt his partner's hand grip his neck in defeat or victory. He couldn't explain it, but he felt right in that water, a space rapturous, ancient with life.

Before each leap, Taoyu repeated a plea. That the water would cure him of his desires. That the impact would clean him, make him brand new.

In everyday life, time isn't agonized over in milliseconds; it can't be slowed down and replayed on a screen as desired. Flicks of water off the end of an eyebrow cannot ordinarily be scrutinized and studied. Not in this life, where moments slip away unnoticed, the second hand braids itself into the minute.

Almost a decade has passed since his last competition, but once in a while Taoyu still gets recognized. Even after he grew his hair out to his shoulders, changed his name, and moved to a third-tier city on the coast.

It can happen anywhere—waiting in line, walking by a taxi's open window—someone will stop him and ask, "Hey, do you and I know each other?" or "I know your face so well, we must have had a drink together before."

No, Taoyu always says no. Tells them they've got the wrong

person. Because if he began his story, he wouldn't be able to finish it. How could he tell these strangers who he is, without revealing who he was and who he had been?

"Name's Peng Hai, *hai* as in the great big ocean, but you're younger than me, so you can call me big brother Hai," said the first boy Taoyu sat next to on the bus. Taoyu's eyes were still sore from crying, but he looked up at Hai's buckteeth and flop of hair and was relieved to have such a happy seatmate.

"I hail from Chang Ping First School. My dad's a railroad worker. My mom's a schoolteacher. I have two sisters and fifteen apple trees," Hai continued. "What have you got?"

Taoyu took in the boy's sand-colored eyes and the flour sack of belongings just like his own. Objectively, he resembled all the other boys he'd grown up with, but there was something friendly and gentle about Peng Hai. A certain kindness in his face that gave Taoyu's heart a tight squeeze.

"One mom and one dad," Taoyu replied, trying to hide the trembling in his voice. Just hours earlier, he had been hiccupping in his mother's arms, begging her not to make him go. "He's not very mature," she had pleaded with Taoyu's father. "Maybe we can wait a year or two and then let him go."

"Out of the question," his father had said. "We're lucky anyone wants him at all."

Older boys pushed through the door and down the aisle, hollering their names at one another as they threw packages of instant noodles across the rows of seats.

"Say, you're awful quiet. Bet you're really smart; quiet kids are always smart. My parents say I talk way too much to have any brains. But I can remember everything. I bet you still don't know which fingernail grows the fastest?"

Taoyu looked down at his hands.

"The middle one! See! I can still teach you stuff you don't know, you should stick with me. I'll be your big brother," said Hai.

"Big brother Hai," Taoyu repeated quietly.

In the end Taoyu suspected even his mother was convinced that this was a cheerful sacrifice. "One day you will need to make it on your own," she had said at the bus stop, her eyes shining. "We all have to leave home someday." Nevertheless, when he had finally let go of her, he still hadn't understood why he had to. It had made him angry with her. What was it he had done?

Oh, to have found someone he liked, to not be alone in this place. What luck! Taoyu thought Hai was the best boy around.

He remembered what the diving scout had said to his parents during tea. "This boy needs to start training immediately with professional athletes." The scout had measured his arms and legs and the skin on his calves. "He is already seven years old, and in a few years he will need to qualify for the regional team."

When the same diving scout had visited Hai's elementary school that spring, he had asked for volunteers for diving and Hai had raised his hand because he loved going to the beach. "Do you think it's too late to change to a different sport now?" he asked Taoyu on the bus. His problem was that he wanted to try all the sports, but he didn't know what they were. What if he was perfect for a land sport, or a team sport, or a sport that hadn't been invented yet?

"Well, they chose me for diving, too," Taoyu said.

"They did? Boy!" Hai said, and his eyes opened up wide. "What are the chances!" He got up on his seat and yelled triumphantly, "Look here! Taoyu here is a diver, too! What are the chances of two divers sitting together?"

An older boy threw a wrapper at his head. They were all there for diving.

It did not seem like an obvious pairing, but as with many simple things that happen at that age, their sitting next to each other on the bus made them best friends. Together they were lined up, measured, weighed, stripped down, and reorganized into individual teams, packs, and disciplines.

Painted in large red letters on the walls was the message they could not yet read: BE POSITIVE, WORK HARD, CLIMB THE HIGH MOUNTAIN, WIN GLORY FOR THE COUNTRY. As their bus drove through the green iron gates of the regional aquatics compound, the boys folded their hands on the windows, the first view of their new life.

With his face pressed against the glass, how could Taoyu have known that his future was shaping itself without his permission, that his genius was ingrained deep in his muscles and bones? How could he have known that the scout was absolutely right about him? That without meaning to, he'd demonstrated something special, and that even though he hadn't asked for it, that very thing was now his responsibility.

Peng Hai had the tendency to find amusement and mischief in the most monotonous routines. If there was a room full of chairs, he would make sure to sit on the table. During study hall, he kept crickets in an empty can and conducted tournament battles under his desk.

Unlike Hai, Taoyu feared for the souls of all the birds that broke their necks flying into the windows of the gym. During the midday rest he worried about the kittens that might be abandoned under the steps of their dorms. For as long as he could remember he was punished for these preoccupations, for his tendency to drift off. In those first weeks he had trouble sleeping. There, in the dark, he was afraid to close his eyes, waiting for some unwanted surprise, and in those moments he wanted nothing more than to call out for his mother.

His mother was the most beautiful woman in the world. As a boy Taoyu was always amazed that when strangers passed her on the street, spoke to her in the market, their mouths didn't hang open with wonder at the sight of her. Anytime his mother called his name, he would go sprinting into her arms, her face cool as a watermelon against his hot little palms. Just being in her presence gave him an immense sense of well-being and he hated leaving her side, even for a moment. Even though he was angry with her now, he missed her.

But without her, there was Hai. Taoyu liked to listen to Hai's ridiculous laugh, which was always the first noise he heard in the morning. He liked to stretch Hai out, always gentle enough not to hurt him. He liked to organize Hai's desk for him and fold his clothes. He even liked just sitting quietly next to him during class before Hai inevitably was scolded for bursting into unstoppable giggles.

Perhaps owing to their fast friendship, Taoyu did not become an outcast. He grew to enjoy the training. He liked the precision of the routine movements as well as the gracefulness of the spins and leaps.

Their world was an incredibly small one; each bit of mischief was hard to come by. In the mornings the boys drilled on the floor mats, first with stretches, then with flips off a stationary board. Then they practiced gymnastics—tumbling, parallel bars, balance beam, and tied to bungee cords diving into trampolines. Two hours of study hall followed by training in the pool until it was bedtime. Much competition was involved in getting a pat of approval from Head Coach Fong, who, as it turned out, had told nearly every boy that he was a once-in-a-lifetime athlete.

Yet when the other boys went home for holidays, Hai and Taoyu were requested to stay behind with their coaches to train and to preserve their concentration. There were not enough hours for boys who showed the most promise.

Once they were assigned as each other's partner in synchronized diving, every moment of their lives was the same. They ate together, picking up their porcelain mugs at the same time. They read together, holding the words to the light with the same tilt of their heads and the matching spread of their fingers. While they lay side by side in their beds, Hai often reached for Taoyu's hand and held it in his own. With their eyes closed they discovered that, hand in hand, even their heartbeats harmonized into a single steady drum.

At first they were afraid of the board altogether, but soon they learned difficult combinations and perfected them during competitions. Initially they felt insecure about the takeoff. Then they couldn't wait to be in the air.

Within the walls of that complex, the days ran by uncounted. Birthdays passed and their adolescent bodies were faithless to their boyhoods. Hai and Taoyu went from perfect boys to elongated ape-men, with angry pimpled foreheads, thick thighs, concave chests, and the raccoon tans of goggles on their faces.

All the boys slept in a single large room with bunk beds so close they could secretly leap from one to the other without the monitors noticing. They fought with one another constantly. They wrestled in teams, pinning one another's throats with their elbows, throwing opponents on their backs and demanding to be called uncle. Sometimes it was savage and that felt good. The room exploded with their musk, surging off their bodies as they explored their strength. By morning, it was not unusual for the sheets to be irreparably stained by a few bloody noses, but nobody ever told. They played horse with socks and a wastebasket. They played catch with marbles or balled-up shorts. Some nights they jerked off. Whoever came last was the loser. No cheating.

The girls slept in another dormitory on the other side of campus. They might as well have been on another planet and they might as well have been goddesses. During the first years it was as if nobody noticed the girls at all, but then the girls became their collective obsession. Every stolen glance was retold, every physical attribute diagrammed, a rare touch on the tumbling mat could become legend. Peng Hai declared his love for Yi Yi, a rower from Jilin, not because she had big pretty eyes, but because she had real breasts and wore contraband nail polish.

Howls rang out after a hand-copied booklet, entitled *The Young Woman's Awakening,* circulated into the boys' dorm. It contained strictly forbidden material. Everyone fought for a chance to peer at the pages filled with medical descriptions of body parts. When it finally made it to Taoyu's bunk, he and Hai dove under their bedspreads to study the booklet under a sliver of moonlight. Taoyu watched Hai's face flush and gasp as he read. Later that night he dreamed about that face, as he often did. Dreams so real he felt shy the whole day after. Sometimes in bed he waited with half-closed eyes until Hai's breath slowed into a murmur, then he reached to feel the hot warmth of Hai's mouth against his palm and pressed it against his own cheek.

There were nights when Taoyu inched close to Hai on their parallel beds. All he knew was that he would have given any-thing to have Peng Hai as his partner forever. Sometimes he was close enough to make out each of Hai's eyelashes in the dark, close enough to touch noses, mouths. There was nothing forbidden about what he was doing, but it hurt, like pressing his fingers on a sprained wrist. On any given night they might be on one side of a bed, just to recount in whispers their day scene by scene. They slept like kittens. Mouth to neck, back to stomach. Knee to bended knee. Mouth to forehead, head to chest. One breath followed by the echo of another. And who's to say if one boy's heart was beating too fast when their hands touched. Or one person was trembling while the other slept. Or maybe in a nightmare, they wrapped their arms around each other, their eyes closed, turning and struggling until the struggling ceased.

His secret desires were perplexing and Taoyu knew only that what he was feeling was wrong. This knowledge overpowered him like a hand to his throat. How long could he hide it from his best friend?

One night, Peng Hai's eyes opened. "Why aren't you asleep? And why are you all the way on my side? What's the matter with you?" he asked sleepily.

Shame and misery took turns with Taoyu. "I'm afraid," he blurted out.

Hai yawned, then adjusted the pillow under his head. "What are you afraid of this time, little bro?"

Taoyu rubbed hard at his eyes to hide his tears. In almost a whimper, he finally said, "I think I'm sick. I'm a pervert."

"Oh," Hai said after a long pause, "oh, I know what's going on." He leaned in to whisper, "Did you . . . did you just wet yourself?" He laughed. "Brother, it's natural! It's just our man engines, gearing up to go."

After Hai fell asleep, Taoyu made a promise to have only chaste thoughts. He wanted Hai to be right. That in some hours, days, or weeks, his engine would catch up with Hai's and they would be the same again.

Before a diver learns how to jump, he must learn how to swim. The ladder will always come before the heights; the fear comes before the water. Before he realized how far he'd come, Taoyu woke up a young man. Fifteen, lean, with broad shoulders and an easy stride, dimensions that made him uncannily perfect for his profession. He and Peng Hai were rising star divers gaining buzz in the athletics community. Competitors from other countries always commented on their consistency. "They're fantastic machines, those Chinese boys. They're just pumping them out year after year. It must be how they're bred."

Taoyu always counted down.

"Ready?" Hai would ask.

"Ready," Taoyu would echo. "Three, two, one."

When walking to the showers, Taoyu stopped looking up at the scoreboard. He didn't have to. The sound of awe followed by the orchestra of applause would always come first.

They qualified for the China national team and the pair was transferred north, to the best sports complex in Beijing.

There, in that new city, Taoyu and Hai blossomed into young men, with rows of hard abs, broad shoulders, and defined jaws. Advertisers began using their images to sell sports drinks, laundry detergent, and motivational CDs.

Together they traveled to Spain, South Korea, and Germany, winning medals all the way. Each time the Chinese national anthem came over the loudspeakers, Taoyu could feel Hai's entire body break out into goose pimples as if they were his own.

Time outside of their fifty-hour training weeks, they could spend any way they wished. The boys' team played cards and drank beer smuggled from the supermarket with the girls from gymnastics. Letters from Ning started arriving underneath their bunk beds. A well-known beauty on campus, she was a star on the balance beam with full heart-shaped lips that she secretly used to smoke cigarettes. Soon Taoyu began helping Hai sneak out of their dorm room after each new letter. He stayed awake until Hai would stumble into bed hours later, dazed and euphoric.

It wasn't long before Taoyu was invited along.

"Ning says she has a roommate that you'd like," said Hai with a shove. "I'm not saying I'm expecting a present, but I'm sure you can figure out a way to thank me for this."

Taoyu didn't think it would be right to miss out on any of Hai's adventures. When Hai held Ning's hand, Taoyu obediently put his arm around Ning's roommate Huan Huan. When the other couple began to kiss, Taoyu did the same, keeping an eye on Hai to make sure he kept up. Then Taoyu would squeeze his eyes shut, tuning out Huan Huan's voice, her toes like cold beans against his legs.

That year a shoulder injury forced Taoyu into a long mandatory rest period. For the first time he was left alone in the dorm room without any drills, and though he was a free man in the capital, he didn't have the slightest clue as to where to go and what to do when he got there. So he wandered around the dormitory in a somber mood, looking for a way to make himself useful.

"Come on, Taoyu," Assistant Coach Yi said on a Friday, "let's get out of here." Yi was dressed in street clothes, with his hair gelled into a point at the front of his head. "Can't just have you walking around trying to sneak into practice."

After sundown Yi drove them to Houhai, the city's oldest party district. Tree-shaded roads wound around still water.

With the music turned up, neither of them had to make conversation as Yi's car wove up and down the streets around both sides of the man-made lake. After a while, Yi turned off the sound and asked if Taoyu had ever snuck out to a party before and Taoyu lied, saying yes, perhaps too defensively because Yi laughed.

"Maybe they went without telling me," Taoyu admitted.

"Hey, it's okay because you're going now."

It was the first Taoyu had seen of this neon maze and he thought he'd never be able to find his way out of it. He watched in awe as Yi expertly maneuvered the steering wheel, the ease with which he reached a bill out the window with two fingers and returned with a pack of cigarettes in his hand. He looked so cool.

"Do you know what Coach Rong is doing now?" Yi asked casually.

"The guys were saying he is an actor?" Taoyu replied. Coach Rong, a former silver medal Olympian, had departed from the training complex the previous summer.

"Is that what he told you guys?" Yi said, watching Taoyu as if to gauge his reaction, which Taoyu tried to keep neutral. "He dances as a woman in a bar. I've seen his act; he's more woman than any real woman. Can you believe that?"

Taoyu nodded at Yi and then sat frozen in his seat. He was afraid to ask a stupid question.

"Men do that, you know," Yi said, winking into the rearview mirror. Then he reached over and placed his arm behind Taoyu's backrest. "Men like you and me. When they get fed up with hiding."

Taoyu stiffened but wondered if not responding would

make him complicit. He felt Yi's fingers on his back and the hair on his neck stood on end. A lure was right there in front of him, but he felt in taking it he would be betraying Hai. At the same time, he wondered if Hai snuck out to places like this.

Yi's car came to a stop in front of a two-story-tall tea club. He could hear the sound of mahjong tiles being shuffled. Just beside the tea club, there sat a low brick building under a neon streak of light, on the far side of the street, shaded by trees. Music was playing inside, the same kind of music that Yi had been playing in the car.

"Is that where we're going?" Taoyu asked, suddenly nervous, as he watched men disappear into a low brick building. Ying turned off the engine.

"It's all right, kid," Yi said, leaving long pauses in between words. "Nobody will know it's you. It's dark."

The first disco made a lasting impression on him even though all night Taoyu stood with his back to the wall. There was not a single woman inside. Coach Yi introduced him to his friends, and these strangers pinched his cheeks and took turns complimenting him. But what Taoyu remembered was their confidence, the ease with which they laughed. They wore thin-soled shoes, jeans, and dress shirts and drank from colorful glasses. Taoyu had his first whiskey, a second, a third.

Before stumbling out of Yi's car, Taoyu asked, "Have you ever taken anyone else to that place?"

Yi leaned over across the front seat so he could see Taoyu's face. "You're so naive, it's adorable," he said with a laugh. "You should watch out for that partner of yours."

"What? What did Hai do?" Taoyu put his hand on the door.

"He's smarter than you, Taoyu. A true snake that one," Yi said. "Let's just say he'll do anything to get ahead."

Taoyu waited, his heart pounding, outside the dorm until morning, when he could slip in unnoticed. A few hours later when he saw Yi, the assistant coach barely nodded at him. The next day Taoyu received a handwritten note tucked inside his locker. It was addressed to "Fresh Meat" and said that the meat was not to his taste but maybe in a few years would ripen and be full-flavored. About a week after Taoyu recovered from his injuries, Yi abruptly left the campus without saying goodbye. They said he moved back to his hometown to get married.

Then it was 2007, a year before China's first-ever hosting of the Olympic games. Something big was about to happen—it had been going on for some time and everyone appeared to be in on it. Ice melted into neat rings. Colors of clothes were more saturated. A plastic sculpture of Mao Zedong in a dress was sold for ten million at an auction. In every kitchen housewives marveled at how plump their rice was cooking. Public displays of excitement were widespread and reactions to one another deadpan. "Let's make an Olympic baby," whispered ten thousand newlywed couples entwined on ten thousand beds.

Apartment complexes, schools, banks, and office buildings were closed up, torn down, and rebuilt into structures that were far more fantastic, more *Olympic*. Enormous digital clocks popped up on the sides of new skyscrapers, on billboards, and on public fountains. Each clock counted down, second by second, to the luckiest numerical configuration in Chinese culture: 888888. The symmetry and promised prosperity of those numbers were in heavy rotation.

It was within the glare of all these epic changes, under these particular falling numbers, that Zhao Taoyu and his partner, Peng Hai, became China's newest Olympic gold hopefuls in 10-meter synchronized diving. Newscasters introduced them on-air to the world as the next legends in springboard diving. Their teenage-boy bodies forever captured on camera, suspended in midair, frozen in graceful gravity-defying postures. If they made it to the podium, people from all around the world would know their impish faces as symbols of youth, physical harmony, and glory.

Before the trials, CCTV aired a special segment featuring the parents of athletes and the sacrifices they've had to make. Walking by a street of small restaurants, Taoyu heard his own name being broadcasted. As he hurried into the noodle shop and up to the television, he recognized the face on the screen as his father's.

"How long has it been since you've seen your son?" the reporter asked.

"Six, no, seven years," his father said. "I haven't seen him for seven years. We don't have the money to travel to see him. Even when my wife got sick, we didn't tell him."

Watching his father's face break up with grief on-screen, Taoyu knew right then that something too terrible for words had already happened. When he thought about it, he couldn't even remember the last time he had heard his mother's voice.

· · ·

In the springtime, his village went wild with willows. One flurry at a time, he liked to catch the pollen expertly between his thumb and forefinger. His mother used to say that it was the girl willows sending love letters to the boy willows. That they were blowing kisses.

Taoyu would happily follow her around the garden as she collected eggs and picked green onions still warm from the sun. In those days she was all his. Then at dusk when his father returned from work, he'd always ask, "What have you two been up to all afternoon?"

"Nothing special," Taoyu would reply and smile at his mom. Even though it was the truth, it would sound like a lie.

The willow seeds seemed to guide his path from the train station toward his house. Former neighbors ran up to him on the street and crowded him, their dialect loud and familiar as they shouted their congratulations. As he neared his house, their voices fell away.

In the years that he'd been gone, Taoyu had grown taller than his father, but the familiar unease of his childhood never left him.

"Your mother got sick while you were abroad and I didn't see the use in worrying you," his father said.

There was a new television on their dining room table. Taoyu did not dare to touch it.

"It was a sudden thing. In the beginning, nobody could say what it was. I didn't want it to interfere with your training." His father placed a hand on Taoyu's shoulder. "Then she ran a fever and stopped recognizing anybody. By then it was too late for you to come home. She wouldn't have even known it was you."

Taoyu looked at his father's face. "You should have told me."

"Even if you had made it back here, it wouldn't have made any difference," his father said, standing up straighter as if he thought the neighbors could see. "You wouldn't have won that medal."

"Just tell me the truth, did she ask for me to come back?" he asked.

"It was too late for you to come back," his father said.

Even if that had been the truth, it sounded like a lie, spoken without love or apology. As Taoyu stood there in the courtyard of his house and listened to his father talk and eventually weep, he was trying to forget him. Forget the particulars of his face, his voice; forget that village that had made him and all the roads that had led him back to this place.

On the train back to Beijing, he felt that his despair was threatening to unhinge him, that if he wasn't careful, he would be lost. It was the longest time he'd been separated from Hai. Taoyu could think only of the muscle that slid from above Hai's heart to meet his neck. The joker smile forever nestled into the corners of his mouth, his waist twisting in the air. Every muscle, each hair he knew and adored. Taoyu wanted to collapse his own body into Hai's, to be held within him.

Taoyu sent Hai's name echoing in the halls of the dormitory. His teammates told him Hai was out bike riding at Peking University, and he ran there to him at full speed. He needed something that only Hai could give him. He knew it was love. Only Hai could replace his wasted heart with his own.

It was dark when he saw Hai through the trees with Ning on the back of his bike, her light blue skirt fluttering behind them like a dragon's tail. Taoyu sprinted after them, crying out, but even though they saw him they didn't stop. Instead they laughed in his direction and Hai pedaled faster. Taoyu stubbornly chased their voices, his breath growing louder than his footsteps.

"Stop! Please," he gasped.

"Not now!" Ning called back, giggling, her ponytail whipping around her moonlit face in the dark.

Taoyu could make out Ning's thin white legs against the spinning wheels, the bike making circles around the trunks of willow trees. Her slender arm was around Hai's waist, and as they passed under the streetlamps, Taoyu saw her bare skin in the dimmed lights. Pale thighs and a gleam of stomach, the curve of a bare white shoulder. He stopped, and when they passed by him again, he saw they were making a joke out of him. Taoyu charged after them, kicking up leaves and dirt.

"See, I told you he wouldn't leave if you told him to, he wants to watch," Ning said, shrieking with laughter, buttoning her shirt together.

"We can talk later, right?" asked Hai. "Can't you see we're kind of busy?"

"Please don't leave!" Taoyu yelled, but Hai turned on his bike and shot Taoyu a weary, annoyed look that sent him running.

"I'm so sorry, brother," Hai said to him later that night, as he moved his hand up and down Taoyu's back. "Death is a part of life, you know. Everyone's parents will pass away. You can't let it break you."

Taoyu put his head down on Hai's lap and wrapped his arms around his waist and sobbed louder. Hai hugged him and Taoyu tucked his legs into his chest. His arms traveled to the soft hairs on the back of Hai's neck, and Hai wiped the tears from his cheeks with his thumb.

"It's going to be okay." Hai repeated it over and over again as if he were using it to keep time. "The coaches were so worried about you. I'm so glad you came back."

They held each other like that for a long while, and for a moment Taoyu dared to think that they were not holding each other as friends, but as lovers. He leaned his teary cheek against Hai's chest and then, reaching up, he lifted his lips to Hai's mouth. With tenderness, Hai kissed him back. Opening his mouth to take in Taoyu's tongue, tasting the tears still flowing down his cheeks. The real and imagined were coming together. It was just like it was in Taoyu's dreams.

Then, abruptly, Hai pushed him away and reached out to look at his wristwatch. "Hey. Don't you think we should sleep now? It's so late and you've missed a lot of practice," Hai asked. Taoyu's body was gasping, his face still red and eager but his partner was perfectly composed.

It wasn't really a question, Taoyu realized. He and Hai, they weren't really the same at all, no matter the beat of their hearts.

Divers have notoriously poor eyesight. It is a hidden cost of the sport and many experienced divers, even with the most advanced eye care, suffer from blurred vision. Yet for the first time in his life, Taoyu saw things for exactly what they were.

What an ingenuous and foolish place he had ended up in, he thought.

During the first day of the Olympic qualifier, a televised event filmed in the newly constructed water cube, Taoyu knew that he could no longer do what was expected of him. The press section clamored to get photos of the duo, and there was never more praise from the coaches. It had taken him months to make sense of all that had happened to him, but it was while facing all those cameras that Taoyu saw a road out. He didn't know it until he stood up there at the edge of the board, when he realized he finally had a choice. Right then, on the world's biggest stage, he could finally choose. He could become a completely new person.

His choice allowed a younger boy to take his place on the team, but Taoyu wouldn't be watching to see who it was. The games would follow in London, then Rio de Janeiro, each with gold medals that had nothing to do with him. By then Taoyu would be living alone for the first time in his life, in a two-bedroom apartment with an ocean view, after changing his name to that of the first cabdriver he had in the new city.

In many ways he had been prepared for Hai to beg him on his knees to stay, following him as he packed, saying, "How can you leave? I'm nothing without you." It was what Taoyu wanted, to disappear from Hai's life completely, to leave a wound that would ache. That was the only way they could be equals.

"Who am I to you?" Taoyu asked.

"You're my best friend!" cried Hai.

How willfully innocent that cruel reaction was, Taoyu thought.

. . .

A few years later, Ning would somehow track Taoyu down at his apartment. She stood there, more striking than ever, knocking on his door until he finally opened it. She had driven all day and night to see him.

"Were you in love with me? I have to know before I get married. Is it because of me that you cut Hai out of your life?"

"No," he replied, and did not explain further, because he didn't owe her an explanation. He wondered if she'd paid the same visit to Hai, who he was told had gotten married and was named Henan's regional sports official in charge of junior soccer teams.

Taoyu would always remember that last jump. "Three, two, one," he could still hear his words echoing from the past. He bent his knees and raised his arms alongside Hai, and realized that they were not going to be together, not beyond that water, not in this life.

He stood still on the edge of the platform, and when the moment came, he did not jump, and traded one life for another. He left all the expectations of his future up there on the board. Instead he watched Hai's body flail underwater, searching for his own. From above, it looked like an elaborate wave goodbye.

The Strawberry Years

ALL OF THIS happened at an otherwise unremarkable period in Yang's life. As often happens when one is learning a new language, in trying not to make an ass out of himself, he was becoming a man of few words. The change suited him fine. He owned just two pairs of shoes and often ate from a bag of expired bread his roommate brought back from bartending. Freelance gigs paid his rent and allowed him to live in a manner that he found comfortable. The only thing worth noting, that stood out at all, was that the woman started appearing in his dreams again.

Stirred by the touch of long, smooth hair against his face, heavy and soft to its ends, he'd open his eyes to see the nape of her slender white neck. From the depth of his sleep, she slowly drew him out by climbing on top of him. He'd gently kiss her palms, her warm throat, but he was never able to quite make out her face. In those moments she could be any girl, an ex-girlfriend even. Facing her in the dark, he'd float his hands to touch her pale breasts and belly.

Soon he would discover, each and every time, that she had two belly buttons. Each a hand's width from the other. He would know right then that it was the same woman and the same dream he'd been having since he was a young boy. He would come right then, like a wounded animal, shuddering onto his thigh, and it would be over.

By the time he'd woken up and tapped open his WeChat, her plane was probably already up in the air, heading in his direction. The short voice messages were coming from a magazine editor for whom Yang had shot some promotional work a few months before. The editor said that there was a famous actress coming from Beijing. It was her first visit to the United States and the girl was alone. Would Yang mind meeting her at the airport and lending a hand to get her where she needed to go? As a small favor to the editor? Her English wasn't great and she didn't have any friends in the city.

Yang could think of nothing he'd rather do less than take the subway to JFK on a freezing January morning. Once you leave China, they say every Chinese person feels like a friend, and the more friends you make, the more roads open up in front of you. But since he moved to New York from Beijing the year prior, way too many people had used him as a volunteer tour guide and translator. Before the editor, it had been his college roommate's nephew, whom he picked up and put on a train to his boarding school. Before that it was his uncle's neighbor's family of three, whom his mother had insisted he treat to a big meal. Still, he couldn't bring himself to say no, and he hated himself for it.

Of all the people walking unsteadily out of the international terminal, blinking into the rows of expectant faces, she was the only one wearing a really big hat. That person, Yang somehow knew right away, was The Actress. The hat was burgundy, with a wide stiff rim, and it fluttered like the wings of a stingray as the person underneath it glided over to him, practically shoving the other passengers out of her way. Though they had never met before, she gave off the impression that they were old friends. Reaching him, she dropped her things and threw her arms around his neck, muffling Yang's face in her citrusy scent. The hat was even bigger up close. Where did she store it on the plane? Yang wondered. Did she have to keep it on for all fifteen hours?

Yang picked up her two suitcases, stacked one on top of the other, and rolled them in front of him. He liked her to begin with; she was pretty in that extraterrestrial catlike way that was in style in Chinese entertainment circles. She had large sparkly eyes, and a small, heart-shaped face with a mouthful of tiny sharp teeth.

"What's the name of your hotel?" he asked as they were walking. "I will take you there before I go to work."

"I didn't book a hotel," she said casually, tucking her arm into his.

"Where are you staying then?" he asked. "Is it like an Airbnb or something?"

"Oh no. I didn't book anything," she replied matter-of-factly. "Was I supposed to pick out a place to stay all the way from China? I've never done something like that before. Everyone only uses WeChat. I don't even have a credit card anymore."

In response to this, he stopped walking, so the actress did, too. He couldn't believe how she could be this calm. What would have happened to her if nobody had come to meet her? They were facing each other in front of the Dunkin' Donuts line, between the taxi stand and the escalators, which led aboveground to the AirTrain. The cold air from beyond the sliding doors blew in Yang's face so that he had to squint to maintain eye contact. Who was this woman? What was he supposed to do with her?

Why had he listened to his messages, why? The editor would have probably found someone else to bother if Yang hadn't replied and none of this would have been his problem.

The actress suddenly laughed heartily even though he hadn't said anything and nothing was funny.

"All right," he said, after taking a deep breath. "I guess you can come to my apartment, use the Internet on my computer, and book yourself a hotel room nearby."

"That sounds perfect," she said, clapping her hands. "How do we get there?"

She dug around in her purse and whipped out her phone, tapping open the video camera and recording herself talking.

"My first train ride in New York City," she said. "So cool! Yeah!"

After he paid for her ticket with his credit card and lifted the actress's luggage onto the train, Yang wondered, Was it him? Was it just that he was so easy to walk all over?

. . .

It was a long ride to Greenpoint. With her phone held aloft in one hand, the actress made a continuous video while chattering on without taking a breath, her physical excitement turning the blank stares of their fellow passengers into a captivated live audience. He could not look away as she talked.

What a dream come true it was to finally be here, considering she'd watched the television series *Beijingers in New York* in the nineties, and each detail on the subway reminded her of a specific scene from the show. Those artists who leave their crummy lives behind to become really poor New Yorkers who go from playing cellos in subway stations to starting enterprising and profitable business ventures. Yet at the conclusion of the series, even though all of the characters ended up wealthy, they were broken and compromised, toasting with champagne in a white stretch limo and one of them standing out of the sunroof with a stupid-looking ponytail flapping in the wind. "What is the point of that?" The actress asked. "So they didn't learn any refinement and ended up as *tu*, as vulgar, as ever?"

She was exhibiting the typical entitlement of those "of-the-moment" Chinese, Yang decided. She casually picked lint out of his hair and blew it off the tip of her finger.

She listed every movie she'd been in and though he recognized quite a few of the names, he could not recall a single scene he'd seen with her in it. "Traditional film industry is over now anyway," she said, brushing off his questions. Now she was pivoting her career to Livestreaming, which she assured him had more viewers and generated more capital than the entire mainland and Hong Kong film industries combined.

"I don't need to wait around for some director to write me

into their dumb script," she said, "I am presenting a version of myself that is entertaining by being genuine and intimate. I have all the power, you know? What I am making is new art."

Judging from her cultural references, they were probably around the same age. Objectively speaking, she was an attractive woman, probably in her late twenties, but in the film industry, at her age she was probably considered some kind of leftover, which couldn't quite explain the hat but did make him feel a tinge of sympathy for her.

When they finally got to his place, a converted furniture store five long blocks away from the Nassau Avenue stop that he'd shared with half a dozen roommates from Craigslist, he handed her the key to his room and gave her the instructions for getting on the Internet. "Nice meetin' ya," he said. "Good luck with everything. Let's keep in touch. Just leave the key in the room when you head out."

Yang was already late for work. One of his roommates inside would have to get her luggage up and down the stairs. She should be able to explain the situation to them. He didn't have time to think what else to do with her.

Work that day turned into a three-day shoot. He was hired to photograph the look book for a wedding dress manufacturer. Not the sort of thing he would ever have taken on in Beijing, but without a work permit, he took any job in New York as long as he was paid under the table, in cash.

Parts of the camera they rented for him were wrong and had to be exchanged. One of the makeup artists didn't show up. They were shooting under the Manhattan Bridge with two assistants holding up a tarp for the shivering and pissed-off Latvian teenager to change behind. Each day was long and exhausting, and the entire crew stayed at a Holiday Inn on the Lower East Side to save time on the commute. Yang barely had a moment to take a proper shit, much less think about the actress. So imagine his surprise when he returned home on the fourth day—exhausted, sore, and with forty pounds of equipment strapped to his back—and even before he opened his door, he heard singing. It was Chinese singing. It was the actress singing!

It was clear that they'd been drinking all day. Four of his roommates sat around their enormous dining table, which was covered with torn-up bags of Asian snacks, with a dozen opened bottles of beer between them. As Yang approached, they immediately wanted him to translate the funny story the actress was at that moment broadcasting.

"What was that? What did she just make me say?" Julian the French painter asked while swaying in his seat like a schoolboy. Richard the bartending saxophonist was blushing from ear to ear next to Jesus, the young kid from Mexico who sold handmade jewelry. Jesus had his arm around his new girlfriend, Gwen, a gangly redhead who carried a plastic harp everywhere she went. Seth was there, of course. Seth who had a website with the description "famous original Brooklyn street artist," who nobody knew what he did all day, and Bryan with his thumb in between a book of Chekhov stories, holding court as usual with his two cats piled on top of each other under his seat.

· · ·

Apparently the actress, with the coordinated efforts of volunteer translators on the other side of the world, had managed to become friends with all of his roommates. She'd shown them fan-made reels across all streaming platforms. With their encouragement she'd set up a makeshift stage, where she'd wrapped a scarf around her head and danced a Mongolian folk dance with the Swiffer as a prop horse. "She has also been cooking everyone awesome Chinese feasts," Julian said with a big smile, adding, "Even better than the stuff you make."

"Oh," Yang said and sat down. Julian placed a plate in front of him. It held a chicken leg.

"You're back already!" the actress said, bringing him a bottle of beer. She hooked her arm around his neck and kissed him on the cheek.

"You look awful," she said. She appeared to study his face closely. "You poor thing! You need to get some rest!"

"I know," Yang replied. After taking a bite of chicken, and speaking Mandarin so that nobody else in the room understood, he said, "I worked nonstop for three days straight. I thought for sure you would have found a hotel by now."

Elbowing Julian off his seat, the actress said, "Well, I was thinking, I want to live here. It's so fun here!"

He thought she was joking. She looked so silly and carefree sitting there next to all his roommates.

"You can't live here," he said. "I live here!"

When he went into his room and flipped on the light, he saw that she had unpacked both of her suitcases and moved aside most of his clothes in the closet. It was only then that it hit him: she was not in fact joking. It was already dark outside and all he could think about was going to bed early. Other friends had joined the dinner theater happening in the kitchen and some of them booed in protest when he led the actress by her arm back into his room.

"Let's figure this out," he said, lowering his voice. "Do you need me to help find you a place to live? I can go ahead and book a hotel room in Flushing for you; they even accept RMB there, maybe even your WeChat money. It won't be a problem."

"It's not that." She took one of his chairs and began turning it in circles. "I just really like the vibe here. It has that, you know, that genuine Bohemian cool."

He looked around at his dim bedroom with its broken wooden chairs and the mattress on the floor. "You don't want to stay here. This is just a warehouse! It isn't even a nice one. It's actually pretty crappy here."

"But I don't mind at all! I really like it!" she said. "This is where real Brooklyn artists live, right? The guys told me they like having me live here and I am welcome to stay in your room as long as I like."

"Which one of them said that?" He couldn't wrap his mind around what was happening. "If you stay in my room, where do I sleep?"

"This room is big enough for both of us," she said. She moved to put her hand on his bicep. "There are already so many people here, what's one more? Now that you're back we can both sleep in here."

She went to close his door with her extended foot and then with a quick twirl she stood smiling at him. "We can sleep together, you and me," she said.

"What? What are you talking about?" asked Yang, standing perfectly still as she slowly moved toward him, slipping off her cardigan and letting it rest in a colorful puddle on the floor.

When he looked up from it, she was already unbuttoning her flannel shirt and revealing the top of a black lace bra. She ripped the last button off the shirt, which up close he recognized to be in fact one of his shirts.

"W-Wait a minute, what are you doing?" he stammered as their arms came together. Usually a woman undressing would arouse him on principle, but her complete disregard for the words coming out of his mouth was frightening.

"Let's just sleep together," she whispered into his face.

"No, that's okay," he said, walking backward into his own table, which had her jacket draped over it.

"Let's do it," she said, shaking out her hair. "I know you want to."

"No, really, I don't want to," he replied honestly. There was something almost chemical happening, he could smell it. It had a smell.

Suddenly she was on top of him, trapping his knee with her crotch. Her sharp tongue licking inside his ear and her ice-cold fingers unbuckling his belt as he tried to buckle it back.

What was happening? Was he dreaming? He had to hold her away from him by the shoulders to make her stop.

"Fine, if you don't want to sleep together, why don't we just sleep beside each other?" she asked impatiently.

"I can't," he said. "I'm a light sleeper."

"I'll be quiet then," she said with narrowed eyes.

"If there is someone else in the room I can't fall asleep," he said, picking his shirt off the floor and pausing to take a good look at her belly button to make sure he wasn't dreaming.

He wasn't and now her perfectly lined eyes looked offended.

"You don't want to sleep with me?" she asked. "So many people want to sleep with me! Almost everybody I meet wants to sleep with me. I am famous! And super hot!"

"You are. I know," he said after a pause. "But I'm not interested" was what he wanted to say, but he was beginning to suspect she was insane. That was a possibility, knowing now that she had not been sent from his unconscious to torment him. "I'm sorry." When she stepped up to him again, he instantly put his hands up in front of his face.

"Who are you to reject me?" she said, poking a hard finger into his chest. "Who do you think you are? What a joke!" She wrapped her arms around her chest and turned her face away from him.

"I just don't want to sleep with you!" he said, looking down as his half-buckled jeans. "I don't know you!"

With her back to him she replied sharply, "Fine. Well, I am going to bed soon, so can you leave?"

He didn't feel like arguing anymore. He was exhausted, his lower back ached, and he smelled like a bag of coins after wearing the same clothes three days in a row. Without another word he left his room, walked down the hall, took a shower, and lay facedown on the lumpy futon in Seth's room.

·　·　·

He had a hard time staying asleep that night. He woke up wanting a cigarette even though he'd quit smoking a long time ago. The molars on the left side of his mouth ached for the first time since he could remember. He sat up in the dark and tried to press the pain away with his palm. Please don't let it be a cavity. He wouldn't even know where to go to find an affordable dentist. The whole apartment was dark and he tried not to wake anybody up as he walked past his room, down the hallway, and into the bathroom. He turned on the light and opened his mouth in front of the mirror. He turned his face this way and that, mouth wide open, looking for something, perhaps a big black hole inside.

Even though Seth wasn't sleeping in his own bed, Yang stayed on the futon out of respect. Seth was probably wrapped around one of the NYU undergraduates he was always meeting online. Yang had been the same way once. Who was that guy who had had such an easy way with women? What had happened to that tall, chill dude with no grievances and nothing to escape from?

Ever since Yang was a boy, the girls on the playground always chose him to swing one end of their jump rope as they hopped around in front of him. But he never understood why, nor did he get why they did some version of it for the rest of his life. He'd be able to stand still for a minute before he got bored and tried to mess with them, trip them, make them fall. Then the girls would report him to the teacher and he'd be scolded, "What girl is going to like you if you do things like that?"

The answer was every girl.

They cheered for him during basketball games, slipped him

cryptic letters in class, and sent him texts late in the night after they were old enough to drink.

How many times had he gone to the adult shop around the corner from his old apartment in Beijing to buy those morning-after pills? While this girl or that girl, with his jacket wrapped around her, stamped her pretty feet on the sidewalk and blew into her hands.

Yang would weigh the colorful plastic packs in his palm "They better work," he said to the shopkeeper. "It's a matter of life and death."

Let the owner glare at him all he wanted, Yang of the past couldn't care less what the old guy thought of him. Then one day they didn't work and his girl got pregnant.

Their son or daughter, if there had indeed been one, would now be going to school. It would be safe to assume the baby's mother went back to working at the accessories stall or that she'd returned home to where she'd come from. Maybe she was doing just fine. Surely there were tracks in the sand that could lead Yang back to that version of himself, though he tried to cover them as best he could.

Deep in his dreams that night, the woman once again visited Yang. There was that familiar pleasure that revealed itself to him, as if he was looking at one of his favorite photographs. The nude body, captured just so, was mysterious and intoxicating. She could bring him just up to orgasm without even touching him. This time he tried to use all his strength to hold the woman up by her wrists, but he could not get her to uncover her face. Two belly buttons. One and then another. She was born once and then born again. Resurrection after resurrection.

. . .

The next morning the actress was in the kitchen like nothing had happened. She was recording Bryan learning how to count up to ten in Mandarin. She'd curled her hair, and her clothes had a vaguely eighties vibe, as if she was starting to take on the apartment's old school aura. There was freshly made porridge simmering on the stove and three roommates had already gathered there waiting with empty bowls.

"So I was thinking about it," she said, her phone's camera pointing at him. She poured some green tea from a kettle and brought it to Yang in a mug. "I think what's best is if I give you money for rent here and you go find somewhere else to live."

Yang put the mug down and took one of the clean spoons Gwen was handing out. Why was she bringing up money? Had the actress been snooping around his room?

"No!" he shouted, startling the other roommates. "I don't want to find somewhere else to live."

"But I want to live here," she said.

"You can't live there. I live there. This is my life," he said, pointing to himself. "There are plenty of other places to live. Please go find your own!"

Turning her chair to face him, the actress explained that her fans loved his apartment. An influential Hong Kong gallerist had started tuning in regularly and even gifted her a coveted cartoon yacht to show his appreciation for her work. Brooklyn life had been one of the most successful twists of her feed. She couldn't just leave now; even he should be able to understand that this was a huge opportunity. She smiled her charming smile and Yang recognized right away that it was the smile that got her favors at airports, free hotel upgrades, and complimentary tickets. The smile that got fans to send her digital flowers, red packets, and diamonds that were adding up to thousands of dollars. He was almost about to agree to something he'd regret when Gwen interrupted them.

"Holiday Inn Express," said Gwen suddenly from the other side of the table. "She's looking for a place to stay, right? Whenever I travel I like to stay at Holiday Inn Express." She held her spoonful of porridge aloft, looked at Jesus as if waiting for his nod of approval. "Only Express though. Because they're like mom and pop owned and have funky themes. Like yeah. They're so great. She'll love it."

"Really?" Yang asked, turning toward her. He felt a profound sense of gratitude. Of course intelligent, sensitive Gwen would come to his rescue.

"Yeah, Gwen loves Holiday Inn Express," Jesus repeated slowly to the actress.

Yang nodded encouragingly at him to continue.

"It's like this ongoing joke between my friends"—Gwen nodded, getting more and more animated—"like, you *loovve* Holiday Inn Express."

"Didn't one of your friends even steal your love of Holiday Inn Express?" asked Jesus. "Like she just pretended your thing was her thing."

"Yeah, she put it on Instagram after I posted about it, about how much she loves it," said Gwen. "But she has, like, way more followers than me." She looked around the table and then added, "She also wrote out one of the recipes I found in *Gourmet* in her own handwriting and then posted it and pretended like it was her recipe and like—"

"Gwen says you will love Holiday Inn Express!" Yang

interrupted in Mandarin, but the Livestreaming audience had already chimed in and the actress's screen came to life with thumbs downs chiming.

The actress shook her head emphatically. "We have those everywhere in China, too."

Yang looked imploringly back at Gwen and Jesus, but they seemed to have lost interest already. He could see that they weren't trying to do him any favors. Yang turned to Seth, who had just walked in the doorway. "Seth, please help me out. I've got to find this actress somewhere of her own to live."

"Sure thing, buddy," Seth said. He winked at the actress, who didn't understand a word they were saying. "I'll be more than happy to take this smoking-hot babe off your hands."

In the afternoon Yang gathered all his dirty clothes and went down the street to the laundromat where the Chinese ladies who worked the wash and fold patted his cheeks when they saw him. They asked whether he was sleeping enough or drinking too much. Yang liked being around them, listening to them talk to one another about their lives. One of them was working to support a husband with lung cancer even though she never saw a doctor for her own limp. The other looked just like his second-grade teacher. Her daughter worked with her on the weekends. Both women had overstayed their visas and were now in the black, undocumented. Yang vowed to make nice portraits of them one of these days, perhaps after fashion week when he could save up enough to focus on the personal projects he'd been neglecting. When he compared himself to these women, his situation with the actress seemed so stupid he could almost start laughing at himself.

That evening when Yang came home from English class, something he had to attend in order to keep up his student visa, he was barely surprised to see the actress still there. She was in the center of the old factory's double-height landing trying to ride the bicycle that Julian, though he would never admit it, had stolen from a memorial for a cyclist hit by a car.

Bryan, completely under her spell, was filming the whole thing.

The actress looked like a newborn calf, her knees buckling out of her torn jeans. Then she straightened up and started pedaling in circles around Bryan with complete ease.

She rode down the hall and into Richard's room and he suddenly stopped playing the saxophone. "What's going on?" he asked, shuffling after her out into the hallway to join them.

"I thought that bike didn't work. Didn't you say there weren't any gears on it?" Richard asked.

Bryan shrugged. "Maybe she fixed it."

Seth was shirtless and lighting up a glass bong when Yang knocked on the door to his room. He smiled at Yang sheepishly through his half-closed eyes.

"What happened, man?" Yang asked. "You said you would help me."

Seth shook his head and moved his hands as if he were juggling invisible balls. "I tried, my friend, I really did," he said, standing up and brushing crumbs off his pants. "I took her to three different places we found together, but she refused to stay in any of them. She said they were all too shitty or something. What was I going to do?" He patted Yang on the back.

"I hated every one of those places Seth took me to," the actress said when he found her lounging comfortably in his room. "The apartments in Manhattan were newer, but these people just wake up, go to the gym, then work all day and don't come back until after dinner. It's so boring."

"Boring?" Yang asked. "It's a place to live."

"I just don't believe that my audience would appreciate it. It's too sensible. This competition for eyeballs is a tough business," she said.

She then put down her phone and her voice softened. "I do feel bad that you insist on sleeping on that terrible sofa," she said, wiping the surface of her phone screen with the palm of her hand. "Are you sure you don't just want to sleep together?"

There were blue, yellow, and black bras hanging on the line that he used for developing negatives. The enormous hat was on the floor in the center of the room.

"Are you crazy?" he asked. "Do you know that this is how a crazy person acts?"

"So what if I am a tad crazy," she said with a gasp. "Maybe you should learn from me, be more crazy! Then maybe you wouldn't just be moping around like a mute, scared of this and scared of that." She held up her phone so that she was speaking directly to her audience. "You know what they say, when everything is easy and smooth, it's dangerous for an artist. You fall asleep on the job.

"Maybe one day you'll thank me for waking you up," the actress announced, half to him, half to her screen. "What do you think, guys?"

He sighed and hot pain seized his rotting tooth. He held his face with one hand and stuffed a week's worth of clean underwear into his backpack with the other.

Against his better judgment, he downloaded the Livestreaming app on his phone. She wasn't exaggerating: the actress really was one of its top users, with hundreds of thousands of active users watching her channel every day, showering her with cartoon Lamborghinis.

There she was pouting on his screen, having changed into a loose wrap dress, streaming from the fire escape just a few feet from him. She earnestly answered her viewers' questions: "Isn't Brooklyn dangerous?" "Do Americans really eat at McDonald's every day?"

The collective commentary of strangers on her message board was clear and knowing.

"Yang is just jealous of you."

"What has he done to make him feel like he deserves this life more than you do?"

"He must be a closet case."

"If he really wanted her to leave, she would have been gone by now. I mean, really."

"Is he attractive?"

"No. Too passive."

"Weak, just like his generation. Doesn't know what he wants."

"Enough already!" Yang wanted to shout at his phone. "Get out of my life! None of you know me! You don't know what I've been through, what I've had to deal with in my life!"

The actress's face popped back on his screen. She was walking briskly down what he could tell was Franklin Avenue. Her candid gaze was different from the one that had emerged from the crowd to greet him at the airport. She no longer smiled. She already looked like a New Yorker.

As he scrolled through the comments aggregated over the course of the last few days, he began to realize that these people talked about the actress as if she were their friend. Even when she turned her camera off, they continued to talk about her among themselves. They knew that both her parents were diplomats and they had left her with her grandparents because they weren't allowed to take her with them. They knew that her mother died of cancer when she was very young and so the actress never knew her at all. Now she dedicated her life to making money and having fun. The viewers defended her. They doted on her, complimented her. They couldn't live without her. Some of them were in love with her.

They said, "She's great. Her whole life. Everything about her."

After an hour Yang had to delete the app. The voices of strangers were like birdsong in a forest, near and then far, and then it became an echo.

That night, Yang tried to sleep under the peeling plaster of Seth's ceiling for what would be the very last time. As he lay awake, he could understand why the actress had come to New

York, a city without parents, and set up camp in his apartment, a place where there was nobody to say "I know you, I know what you're capable of. What kind of person you are."

After a while he decided to go buy some cigarettes. There was music playing in the kitchen, but he went straight for his winter coat, hanging by the door, and ran down the stairs. Outside he could hear the train rushing to a stop in the distance, screaming as it approached the few bundled-up passengers backing away from the noise. He walked on new snowdrifts, freshly settling on the sidewalks, and past small piles of snow with cars underneath.

By the time spring comes perhaps the actress would still be living in his room. On weekends the actress could go sell bracelets with Jesus near the Prince Street subway and on weekdays she could attend the same English classes as he did in the financial district. Maybe Bryan would ask her to do some translation for his independent press, and when her English got good enough, maybe she'd start going to all those Broadway auditions with Julian's boyfriend. Any tension and unhappiness will have been neutralized and the only person it would inconvenience would be him.

At the deli, Yang purchased a pack of American Spirits and a lighter. The first inhale made him dizzy and he had to lean his back against the shop's advertisement-covered windows. The streetlights illuminated the shapes of the industrial chimneys in the distance, which so closely resembled the factories he used to play inside of as a boy. Come to think of it, they were nearly identical to the warehouses in Changchun that he and his friends had broken into for fun, bursting out to tag one another, stepping on broken glass, nails ripping their winter coats. The site managers were always after them, but the boys and girls scattered into the dark corners, giggling, escaping the reach of grown-up hands. Yang was never trying to get into trouble. He just wanted to extend each minute of time, before the sky got dark, before it inevitably started to rain and playtime was over.

Just then three girls turned the corner, all of them in a festive mood. Their voices hushed to a conspiratorial octave as they passed him. One of them came up from behind Yang and draped the soft sleeve of her suede coat over his neck.

"I think you should come with us to this party," said the girl, her eyes blue like glaciers, her mouth sweet with whiskey. "Isn't he hot, you guys? He's so hot, right?" she asked her friends, who tried to drag her away. The blue-eyed girl was still holding on to his hand and he was about to ask "Where is the party?" but the words came to him in Chinese.

Then like a voice in an interrupted dream, they flew out of him in perfect English.

TIME AND SPACE

Algorithmic Problem-Solving for
Father-Daughter Relationships

TO BE A leader in the field, every computer scientist first needs to understand the basics. Back away from the computer itself and into the concepts. After all, a computer is just a general-purpose machine; its purpose is to perform algorithms.

It is due to the fact that algorithms are unambiguous, that they are effective and executable. However, algorithms aren't just for machines. In designing an algorithm, a person can execute a complex task through observation and analysis. To be a good father, it would be a logical assumption that these same acquired skills should apply.

As I used to say during my lectures at Heilongjiang University some thirty years ago: Everything in life, every exploit of the mind, is really just the result of an algorithm being executed.

For example: To peel garlic
Obtain a bulb of garlic and a small plastic bag
As long as there is garlic, continue to execute the following steps:
1. Break the garlic petal from the garlic bulb.
2. Peel off the outer skin.
3. Place the smooth garlic into the bag.
4. Throw the skin into the wastebasket.

To my students and colleagues I once famously said the same can be applied to something as complicated as getting married. As long as an adult male is still without a wife, continue to execute the following steps:

1. Ask librarians, family members, and coworkers if they know any single girls.
2. Invite girls to watch movies.
3. Assess compatibility facts as follows:
   a. Beauty
   b. Family
   c. Education
   d. If compatibility measures up to previously set standard, move to step 4; if not, start from beginning.
4. Ask the girl to be your wife.

A librarian introduced me to my ex-wife. Her nose was too small for her face, her hairline too high. However, she came from a family with good Communist party standing and we attended similarly ranked universities.

One day, on the way to see a play, she lost the tickets and I yelled at her for her carelessness. I thought that was the end of us. Then on our way back, I stopped along the street and tied an old man's shoes for him. She agreed to marry me after that.

There was a miscalculation in this equation, which I now see, of course. I liked the girl I married very much, but not the woman she became after we immigrated to America. This woman never respected me. All the data was there to be sorted, I just didn't decode it until it was too late. She had this way of making me feel spectacularly incompetent. She was a literature major in college and she had what people said was a good sense of humor. Once I took her to a company party and all anybody could talk about the next day was how ravishing my wife was. That was when it began to bother me. That people didn't think I deserved her. That they thought I was somehow less than her.

I don't think she understood the protocol of being a good wife. "Let's go into the city and eat at a nice place," she used to say. Why? So I could feel more out of place for not being able to read the menu? No, thank you.

But without her, there would be no daughter, Wendy. There's that to consider.

Now that I'm older, I see that my theory proves itself day after day. Until illness and then death, life is indeed the outcome of algorithms being performed. I didn't need a coach to learn how to play tennis, because before I even stepped on the court, I understood the fundamental math of the game using an algorithm. I know that the GPS in my car is using another algorithm, taking its calculations to a satellite to tell me where my car is.

So right now I need to make a new algorithm to solve the problem of Wendy. My only daughter, who I somehow managed to drive away from me—door slamming and eyes pooling up during dinner.

I wish to concentrate on the relevant details of our relationship from tonight and beyond in order to break down our problem into something that can be decoded, processed, and used to save our relationship. How did I hurt her? Will she ever come back to me?

This evening was one of those calm, snowless December evenings in Westchester County. My daughter, whom I hadn't seen in nearly a year, was home on vacation from studying in England and planned to spend two weeks living in her old bedroom. I had already prepped the pigs' feet to throw in the pressure cooker and defrosted tofu skins I'd smuggled in from my last trip to Jilin. When she walked through the door, pink nosed and taller than I remembered, I felt such a rush of affection for the girl that I went right up to her and pinched her arm really hard.

I broke down these two weeks into pseudo code just to see how it was going to work out in my mind:

If (daughter comes to stay) then (if [temperature = cold])
   then (enjoy home cooking)
   else (watch movies)
   else (buy her consumer electronics)

"Baba, is it your goal to make me obese?" she asked when I showed her the five-pound bag of uncured bacon shoved in my fridge. I replied, "Oh, come on, little fatty, you know you crave my pork stew," and she laughed. She hadn't changed very much, had the same soft chubby hands that I love squeezing. She still had my smile, the one that was all gums.

Even before I had finished putting out all the vegetables and meats on the counter for prepping, Wendy was already showing me pictures of all her weekend trips. She'd been to France, Italy, and Spain. I pulled my head back so that the countries came into focus.

"Where are pictures of you?" I asked as she clicked.

"I was too busy documenting the landscape." She went through the snapshots slowly, importantly, lifting her computer to show me pictures of bus stops, lampposts, jars of pickles.

"How do you have so much time to travel when you're supposed to be studying?" I asked.

"You think I went all the way to England just to sit in my room? Besides, all the Brits do it, too."

For me, she spoke Mandarin, which had gotten rusty. She mispronounced words and made up her own metaphors. But I loved hearing her talk, just like when she was a child, telling me stories while I tried to teach her how to make a good steamed fish. While her mother would be out taking real estate courses or painting a still life, Wendy would always keep me company in the kitchen. I didn't want to look at the pictures, but I was happy having her voice fill up the house. I gutted a red snapper and stuffed it with ginger.

"Can't say I have the same attitude toward education," I said. I handed her a potato peeler and she finally put away her laptop.

"Of course I study, too, Dad, I study all the time. I've made a ton of friends from all over the world," she said.

"That's good, expanding your horizons," I said.

"There are Chinese students at my school, too. Bunch of wackos. They just stay in their dorm rooms and make dumplings all the time. It's fun, I guess, but *all* the time." I nodded, and she went on. "In England. Can you believe that?"

"And they are your friends, too?" I asked.

"No, they don't talk to me. Probably because I speak English and don't study engineering." She started slicing the carrots into strips, and I showed her how to make them into stars. "But I didn't go over to England to pretend like I lived in China, you know?"

"Probably good you aren't friends with them," I said solemnly. "The only Chinese kids who get to study in England have to come from crooked families with embezzled money."

"Maybe . . . but I can't imagine it would be all of them," she said, squinting at me. "There was this one crazy thing that happened while I was there. There's a lake in the middle of campus where the university raises exotic geese from all over the world. Then one day the caretakers noticed that one of the Egyptian geese was missing its mate."

She stopped talking until I gave her my full attention. "Turns out this Chinese student had killed it! Goose dumplings." She put down her chopping and with great effect said, "The university expelled him."

"That's a pity."

"Isn't it? I heard the guy was from Anhui," she said. "And I just kept thinking, why did he do it? Even if he didn't know they were pets. What made him see a magnificent bird and immediately want to kill it?"

"I wouldn't worry about it, Wendy," I said. How could she know that my brothers and I used to kill sparrows with slingshots in order to eat them. How we shot so many sparrows the birds couldn't land and became so exhausted they began falling out of the sky, dead.

"It's just so typical of Chinese people, too, not to even protest their friend's expulsion." She went over to the sink and peeled with great indignation.

If anything, I thought, it was she who protested too much. Always concerned with things that she had zero control over. Like missing her SATs for a hunger strike against the Iraq war, something she had nothing to do with.

I could have told her about the look on my baby brother's face when he reached the bottom of his bowl of cornmeal gruel and I gave him the roasted sparrow. Our teeth were worn down from eating that gruel and we were never full. Maybe then she might have understood. But the water came to a boil and the fish had to be steamed.

Then there was the wine.

"I brought you this wine, Baba, carried it on my back through three border crossings," she said. "It's from Ravello, below Naples, on the way to this scenic town called Amalfi." I nodded at the unlabeled bottle, which was made of heavy green glass.

"It was a family vineyard. The vintner said it was the best

wine he's ever made. The vines grew on the cliffs facing the ocean. I had to hitchhike just to get this bottle for you." The girl kept going excitedly, her hands remembering Italy.

Right then the phone rang. It was Charles and Old Ping, my two divorced and now bachelor buddies. They were wondering what I was doing for Christmas dinner. These buddies and I cut one another's hair once a month. They had nowhere to go that night, so naturally I invited them over.

"Come! We are going to have great food—and Wendy's here," I said.

I smiled at Wendy and she shrugged and went about opening the wine. She couldn't have been upset about that, could she? Having my best friends over to share our Christmas dinner? Surely she wouldn't be that selfish. In fact, even though she's not very logical, she was always a remarkably reasonable, well-behaved child.

My ex-wife and I, we never hide things from her; she shared equal partnership in the family.

Maybe there were some things we shouldn't have told her. She probably shouldn't have been at the lawyer's during the divorce agreement where I probably shouldn't have yelled at her crying mother, "What are you going to actually miss? Me or the money?" That was probably a mistake, but I can't do anything about that now.

Was it the wine? I bet it had something to do with that wine. As we were preparing the last of the food, we had a rather unpleasant conversation about the fundamentals that make up a good bottle. "The most popular cocktail in China right now is the Zhong Nai Hai #5," I said. "They say it was created by former premier Jiang Zemin himself, wine with Sprite."

"Ba, let me tell you some of the basics. So the most common red wines are merlot, cabernet sauvignon, and Syrah," she said. She continued on like an expert. "Wine is not supposed to be *ganbei*-ed, the way you do it. It's supposed to be tasted and sipped, since it's about the appearance, the smell, the aftertaste. Try!"

"That sounds like a needless hassle to me," I said. "It's a drink."

"You know, you were probably destined to be a lonely migrant farmer, but instead you were blessed with me, and you don't even know how to appreciate it!"

She circled the kitchen counter and stood facing me. "Come on, I thought you'd like knowing about this," she said as she slowly opened the bottle. "While I'm here, maybe I can take you to a wine tasting in the city. It'll be really fun!"

"You can save your energy, Wendy. Your old baba is not fancy, and I'm not going to stick my nose in there like a pretentious snob. I have always been a simple guy, in case you forgot," I said with a sniff, "while you were in Europe."

I took a sip from the glass she poured for me and said, "I feel that in my experience, the best wine is wine that is over fourteen percent alcohol content, in a bottle with a wide neck, and preferably that bottle should have a large indent at the bottom."

I thought I saw her roll her eyes at me, so I said, "When did you get so stuck up? Did you learn that from your mother?" And she turned away from me.

The previous situation can be broken down into pseudo code as:

If (daughter is frustrating) then (compare her to her mother)

While (daughter shuts up) do (change the subject)

When the doorbell rang, Wendy skipped over to answer it and I assumed everything was back to normal. She was very polite to both of them, like a good daughter. I didn't even have to ask her to unpack the two cases of beer into the fridge. What a sight my friends must have been to her! Old Ping was as unwashed as ever, but he had at least changed out of his work overalls for the occasion. Charles still had paint splatters above his eyebrow and his hair had grown long everywhere that was not bald.

When I tried to offer them Wendy's wine, both of them initially refused.

"I don't know about foreign liquors. Most things white people like give me the runs," said Charles.

"I'll stick to my *baijiu*, but thanks, young Wendy," said Old Ping, whose eyes were already rimmed with red. He must have started drinking in the car.

Wendy set the table while I finished cooking. It was one of my most sumptuous spreads. There were five dishes, fish done two ways, and a soup. All the colors satisfied, every plate still hot. Old Ping opened twelve bottles of beer and clinked them against the plates. Now we could eat.

·   ·   ·

"A toast," Old Ping said, "for young Wendy giving us the honor of her presence. We owe it all to you for this nice meal we are having."

"Don't pay attention to your uncle Ping, he has no education like you," said Charles.

Old Ping pointed a chopstick at Wendy. "Be nice to your old dad, don't neglect him."

"*Chi, chi!* Eat, eat!" I said, digging into the brisket.

The table was quiet with eating until Ping started talking again. "Say, Wendy Wendy Wendy, when are you going to get married?"

"Ah, don't bother the girl, Ping, she's going to get a Ph.D. Isn't she?" Charles asked me.

"You know!" Old Ping cut in. "They have a saying in China, there are three genders: men, women, and women with Ph.D.s."

"Well, this isn't China, last time I checked," she replied.

"Don't take too long, is my advice," said Old Ping. "Make sure you find a boyfriend before your Ph.D. scares all the boys away!"

I jumped in. "She doesn't have to worry about that. If she doesn't want to get married or can't get married, or whatever, she can always live here with her old dad. I'll pay the bills."

Then what the heck, they decided to give the wine a shot. Charles asked her, "Wendy, you really think this tastes good? I'm not going to lie. I'm ignorant."

"It's from a family vineyard in Italy," I said. But not wanting to make my friends feel out of place, I added with a laugh, "Not that *I* could taste the difference."

"It's a smidge too sweet," Old Ping said as he wobbled toward my refrigerator and cracked a few ice cubes from the ice tray with his hands. He sauntered back to the table with a fistful of ice cubes and I reached out my glass.

I drank a big gulp and gave a satisfied sigh.

It happened sometime after that. Charles had made us all take some shots of *baijiu* and we were still cracking jokes when I noticed Wendy had stopped eating. She pushed her bowl away from her and was blinking at the ceiling light.

"Have some fish," I said to her.

Her eyes glistened. "Dad, why am I here?" she said, getting up from the table. "I flew back just to spend time with you, but it's like you don't need me at all. You have no interest in me. It's like I'm . . ."

"Oh, so if you're going to have to spend time with me, it should be all about you."

"I'm not saying that."

"*I* should be honored that you came back."

"Jessica's dad said her first verb was 'scurry'! What was my first *verb*?" she asked me.

"How am I supposed to remember a word from twenty years ago?" I laughed. I should have just made something up on the spot, like "eat"! "Don't be a brat, Wendy, we have guests here."

"Come on, calm down," Charles said. He had his own grown daughter that he was afraid of.

Knocking against the table, she struggled to put on her jacket. "Hey, you can't be mad at your dad," I said. "I raised you, you can't just throw a tantrum over nothing." Somehow I accidentally ripped a few hairs from her head in trying to stop her from putting on her jacket and getting up.

She yanked away from me and went into the kitchen. I got up and the ground moved below me.

"Think of all the stuff I bought you. Think of all the sacrifices I've made for you. Now you come home with a bottle of wine and ask me questions? Make demands on *me*?" I said, yelling now. "Do you know how much of my money it cost to raise a bratty girl like you all these years?"

She stopped by the kitchen door and looked at me. "You calculated the exact amount of money it cost to raise me?"

Old Ping cleared his throat. "Hey, Ma, stop it now."

"Yeah, it's one hundred and fifty thousand U.S. dollars not including all your tuition," I said to her, the blood rushing to my head like I was hanging upside down. "How about I act like Jessica's American dad and ask you to pay me back?"

She stared at me through narrowed eyes, shaking with rage.

"Yeah, why don't you pay me my money back?" I said as I banged my hand on the table. "Why don't you think about that?"

She didn't even bother to close the kitchen door on her way out. Charles and Old Ping followed soon after that, too, leaving the table a mess of bottles and bones. An hour passed before I realized she was not going to take responsibility for her disrespectful behavior and return to apologize. Fine, let her have it her way. If she was going to be disrespectful and ungrateful, then that's her code of operation. I don't get it. My mind works best in bytes, in data, in things permanently and irrevocably true. I'm not even going to pretend that I understand women at all.

It's possible that I might have said some things in bad taste. I might have drunk slightly too much as well. Thus, I had a problem on my hands.

I am aware there are limits to the capabilities of the human mind. That's why solving complicated algorithms is difficult; it requires a person to keep track of so many interrelated concepts. The solution couldn't possibly be figured out that very night. The last of the wine tasted bitter in my mouth, but I drank it anyway. Birds went up into their nests and I went to bed.

Wendy didn't call that night. She is still young, self-important, and takes her hurt feelings seriously. Even though she knows, or at least should know, that I'd simply lost my temper. But even though I am asleep in bed, things will start happening. That's the phenomenon of problem-solving; the mysterious wells of inspiration will often follow a period of incubation. Often the most difficult problems are solved only after one has formally given up on them.

So while I sleep, my mind will be calculating. The subconscious part of my brain will continue working on a problem previously met without success. Even after I wake up, work my joyless eight-hour shift on the assembly line at the Hillsborough computer repair shop, then watch basketball with Charles and Old Ping, I'll be subconsciously trying to get to the mysterious inspiration to solve my not-yet-unfathomable problem. Once I do, the solution will be forced into my conscious mind.

· · ·

Everything makes logical sense in computer science. Computers know not to get sentimental; they can rise above it and work in symbols and codes. The world of imagination, uncertainty, and doubt can be managed through entities and hex notations, and sooner or later everything becomes representational and quite manageable. You don't need to worry about the specifics once you figure out the abstract.

My favorite is the nondeterministic polynomial, which is simply a case in which someone or something, a magic bird perhaps, shows up out of nowhere and gives you the "answer" to a difficult problem. The answer is "yes." The only thing you need to do is find a way to check if the answer is correct, that the circumstances of the problem actually exist, and be able to do so in a reasonable amount of time.

At one point in the past, I thought I had all the answers already. It happened before I moved to America, before the marriage, before the daughter, before I even attended college. It was the summer I hitched a train to Guangzhou, then bought the cheapest ticket to Hainan. I was eighteen years old with a shaved head and twenty yuan in my pocket, but I just wanted to see the ocean, to float above the water and see the sand below. I still remember it now, that water reflecting a million perfectly placed petals, lifting up to meet the moon. Those birds that lined the trees like big white fruit, who transformed back into birds when I approached them, and flew away to become clouds. Those clouds reaching down to meet the sea, like a lock of wet hair on a girl's neck.

It was then that I realized that the reflection of the water on the sand looked like the electricity in a light bulb, like the mysterious maps of marble. I thought I knew the answer to a question I hadn't even asked, that there was some order in this universe.

Life happened so quickly. My hair thinned and I developed a paunch. The years melted and quietly pooled at my feet. Before I was at all prepared, I was married to an ambitious woman, with a precocious daughter, giving up my professorship and moving to New Jersey to become another immigrant American living an ordinary immigrant life.

Now that I think about it, those years were like watching a sunrise. It was not at all like the pleasant vision I'd had in mind. It was too much to fathom, the great sun peering out from the distance: warm and comforting for a moment and then brilliant, too brilliant to bear. The soft halo of light quickly became a flare and it stung. And yet, by the time I learned to turn away, most of my life was over.

Some nights I wake up in a panic and wonder: Why did everything that I worked for turn into what I despised? How did I become an old man? How did I end up with no one?

Algorithm discovery is the most challenging part of algorithmic problem-solving. The phases themselves are unambiguous, but it is *determining* them that is the art. To actually solve a problem, I must first take the initiative.

Phase 1: Define and understand the problem.
Phase 2: Develop a plan for problem-solving.
Phase 3: Execute the developed plan.

Phase 4: Evaluate the solution for accuracy, and for its potential as a tool for solving other problems.

PHASE 1: DEFINE THE PROBLEM: THE DAUGHTER HERSELF

I always knew this daughter was going to be trouble. The first inkling of it was sparked when I used to take her on my bike around my old campus. Because we didn't have any children's seats, I sat her on the pole directly behind the handlebars of my bike. The first thing I told her was to never, ever put her feet close to the wheels. They would get caught and the wheel would cut her feet badly.

So the first thing she did was get her feet caught in the wheel. Cold sweat beaded my face as I bandaged her bloodied little feet, but she barely cried. It was as if she was testing me. It was as though she went against my warning just to be sure I was telling the truth.

Phase 2? No, let's go back.

PHASE 1: UNDERSTAND THE PROBLEM: IMMIGRATION

Maybe it began soon after Wendy was born, after my wife and I boarded a plane from Beijing to JFK. Probably right after I took my first bite of a ham and peanut butter sandwich and liked it. The problem might have arisen following decades of listening to the same Chinese songs, driving to Queens to be surrounded by other transplanted Chinese people, craving the same food we left behind. Perhaps it was sparked during the last twenty years of watching American TV, how I could never understand enough of the dialogue to chuckle along with the laugh track.

Phase 2: Could it have begun because TV wasn't funny? No, let's try again.

PHASE 1: UNDERSTAND THE PROBLEM: UNFAIR AND UNEXPECTED REVERSAL OF ROLES

When I pictured myself being a father, I'd always assumed I'd take the lead in the relationship. I'd teach her how to read, how to ride a bike, how not to talk to strangers, all of that, but a lot of these opportunities at fatherhood were co-opted from me. It was she who taught me how to read English, when she was eleven. When she was twelve, she helped me pass my citizenship exam by making up acronyms. When she was sixteen, I taught her how to drive, but it was my daughter who filled out the forms to renew my license. I never got to console her over some punk boy breaking her heart, but she held my hand when I cried after her mother left me.

Is that all there is? It can't be. Cannot proceed to phase 2.

I must admit, there are ultimately some limitations to algorithms. A difference does exist between problems whose answers can be obtained algorithmically and problems whose answers lie beyond the capabilities of such systems.

A problem solved algorithmically would be my temperamental attitude. I have since stymied the urge to physically threaten teenage boys being assholes in public and I no longer pay for car damage due to routine road rage. It was logical reasoning.

However, there is a line to be drawn between processes that

culminate with an answer and those that merely proceed for-ever without a result, which in this case might be:

1. The problem of wine
2. The problem of daughters

I can't give up. There has to be a solution. Wendy and I used to have a good relationship, a great relationship, with some all-involving grace that didn't need problem-solving. When I watched her ride away on her first bicycle, her ponytail flapping back and forth like a bird's wing, or as I listened to her sing in the school choir, my heart skipped when she spotted me in the crowd and waved. That's my girl! I made her! Like when I visited her third-grade open house and she showed me that in her bio she had written "hiking with father" under hobbies and "father" under heroes. That's got to be worth something.

A portion of my unconscious mind will go on translating ideas from abstraction to pseudo code and laying it out systemi-cally in algorithmic notations. It will be an ever-slowing pro-cess. Once I wake up, life will bring about more arguments and disappointments; small trespasses in this long life to live.

My relationship with my daughter might never fully re-cover from this night. We might miss a lot of holiday cooking together, and my hair will thin even more, and she will grow just a tiny bit taller. Maybe out of the blue, some years from now, she will introduce me to a boyfriend, a strange-looking but polite boy. It might take even more years, but maybe she will come home and apologize and wash my dirty pillowcases and overeat in order to please me. I wouldn't be able to know how unhappy I had been until she returns.

She cannot abandon me. She loves me and thus will be able to anticipate my indignation and put my hurt feelings before her own. Those are some of the concessions made. There will be others. These sequences of instructions are programmed within her; that is her heritage.

Ah, but the solution, and there is one, will come to me years later. Perhaps when I am on a fishing boat in Baja, or in the middle of my honeymoon with my second wife, or in the hospital room at the birth of my new baby daughter, Lana. When it comes to me, and it will, I will remember this:

One afternoon, not long after we immigrated, when my daughter was still growing out of her baby teeth, I came home from work early and found her walking alone around the dim apartment. Holding a hand mirror faceup at her waist, she walked from room to room while peering down into the reflection.

"What are you doing?" I asked.

"I am walking on the ceiling," she replied.

I was about to tell her to stop fooling around, to do her homework, but instead I paused and allowed myself to go with her imagination instead. I tried to picture what enchanted beasts she might have up there walking on the ceiling with her. She still had those worried dark circles under her eyes back then and my love for her was still simple and pure. This is what I need to tell her. Not her first verb, but this, the moment I realized she was better than me. She would have both sides of this world, the whole thing.

Echo of the Moment

THAT MORNING, JUST before 9 a.m., Echo stood on the landing with her hair combed and her tennis shoes on, waiting for one of her neighbors to open their door. After four weeks of living in her rented apartment, she was determined to meet someone. When the wooden floors creaked across the hall, Echo pretended to take out her garbage and met a tall, angular woman named Anne-Laure.

They did the *bisou* on both cheeks. They did not ask about each other's lives. They only exchanged low-level smiles, the kind you reserve for the cashier at Monoprix when you're buying one item in a hurry. "*C'est un batiment tranquille,*" Anne-Laure said slowly and politely, "everyone keeps to themselves." But that wasn't true at all; Echo could hear Anne-Laure's music and smell her hashish. Echo thought that if she could, she would pass through her walls and emerge through Anne-Laure's picture frames into her living room and touch her soft, sparkling things.

Echo had not even finished locking her door when Anne-Laure was already one flight down. She stood there still holding her garbage, hoping to meet another neighbor when her cellphone rang.

It read Celine.

"Echo, what size clothes do you wear?" asked Celine in her trademark New York accent, not pausing for a breath. "Like the smallest, right?"

"What?" Echo asked.

"Do you know what size clothes you wear?"

"Not sure exactly, it depends." Echo had never cared much about her clothes. "Why?"

"Look at something you're wearing, quick," Celine said, her earring making a clipping sound into the phone. "Are you a size zero or what?"

"Zero," Echo repeated, even though she hadn't looked. "Sounds about right." She looked down at her flat chest, the noodle legs that made her jeans ride up and the arms that were mostly elbows.

"You know how you only own, like, one pair of pants?" Celine asked. "And how you're still wearing that hideous jacket you found in a movie theater?"

Echo didn't know how Celine knew about this.

"So here's the thing," Celine continued. "I'm going to hook you up with some free clothes. Pretty much new, really high-end stuff. You just need to come to one of my units at Rue Chapon to pick it up yourself."

"Oh," Echo replied, sensing there must be more to this story. "Why are they free?" she asked. "Is there something wrong with them?"

"Nothing is wrong with them. You just need to come now before the police come back and clear everything away." There was a pause before Celine quickly whispered, "Just don't tell anyone about this."

Echo lowered her voice as well. "Is this, like, stealing?"

"God, no!" Celine said, and paused again, as if she was trying to explain some cultural anomaly. "Look, the girl who owned the stuff killed herself two days ago—don't worry, she didn't do it in the apartment; she jumped in front of a train. Luckily, I manage her building and saw that all her clothes are just sitting there in her apartment. You have to come and take some. Who knows where it will all end up otherwise?"

"Celine, I . . ." Echo started, but Celine interrupted by repeating the address for her to write down.

"Just come and see the clothes before you say no! I mean, the girl's already dead."

Her mouth was open, but Echo felt the appropriate time to refuse Celine's offer had come and gone. Plus, she had been looking to change certain things about herself and perhaps this was all part of the plan. "Okay," she said after a long pause, "I'll . . . come."

A month prior, Echo had met Celine by chance. Celine's office was next door to the upscale tourist destination L'Ami Louis.

The agency was staffed entirely of loud, curvaceous older American women whose job it was to assist foreigners in finding long-term rental apartments in Paris. The two ex-mistresses, a former trophy wife, and a trio of forever-emerging artists on staff were known for their taste, attention to detail, and warmth.

When Echo, a shivering twenty-one-year-old Chinese American girl, stumbled in from the rain, alone and after having just been pickpocketed on the sidewalk, Celine stepped out from behind her desk and gave her a big motherly hug. "You're still going to have the best time in Paris," she cooed. "So you lost your passport? There are still churches, there are still cafés, and there are sculptures that will wink at you every time you walk by."

From then on, every once in a while Celine would call Echo, who would inevitably be wandering around the city avoiding her French studies. Over coffee, Echo would listen to Celine talk about her love life and where to eat the best *chaussons aux pommes*. As she listened, Echo would feel herself passing temporarily into a new world. A world without anxiousness, without dread. A world free of her own depressing thoughts.

Toward the farthest corner, between the freight elevator and the trash bins, was where Celine told her to wait. So that's where Echo waited, even though the sour stench lifting off the bags gave her the shivers. She held her breath and swiped at her phone's screen until she heard footsteps and saw Celine's pale white calves emerge from the dark like teeth.

"Oh, darling, don't look so scared," Celine said as they hugged and a puff of perfume escaped from her collar. "This is not even a big deal!" She waved half a dozen blue IKEA bags in Echo's face.

A week ago, a red-eye flight from Kuala Lumpur to Beijing had hypnotized the world by vanishing without a trace. Day after day helicopter cameras focused on large swaths of ocean or, rather, focused on the boats tugging side-scan sonar devices under the waves. Viewers were asked to imagine, beneath the blue water, fiber-optic cables combing the seabed for debris. Perhaps that was why none of the neighbors saw Echo and Celine approach the door to apartment 29. Behind their closed doors, they, too, were mesmerized.

As Echo followed Celine's skirt up the stairs to the third floor, her footsteps reverberated down the hallway, drowning out the sound of her own thumping heart. The door was blocked off with two lengths of red tape and a police seal on the door.

"In here," Celine whispered, waving her hand impatiently. "You're going to lose your mind when you see this stuff." She ducked under the tape and leaned against the door, which swung open with a soft click, and nearly without thinking, Echo followed.

Experts in the fashion industry say the first clothes that people are drawn to are instinctual. Think of your favorite clothes as a child. Then as you mature, you focus deeper into the self. Now you favor clothes that involve sexuality, yours and other people's. You begin to reflect your profession, your mental state, then address your personal affectations. Your personhood. And then you start to look into the world. At society and history and nature. You feel for texture and you create contrasts and distance.

It wasn't the quantity but the particularity of the clothes that stunned Echo. Floor-to-ceiling shelves were stuffed with sweaters of supernatural textures, warmed by the daylight that poured through the open windows. Shoes lined the edges of the room, facing the center, like a fabulous invisible audience. On one wall, there were racks of dresses one on top of the other, arranged by color. They introduced themselves to Echo, teaching her this and that about themselves.

An armoire of vintage cashmere coats was organized around a set of themes. This suede that felt like velvet recalled the fashions of an ancient era, while the leather referenced the recent past. A silk gown in a glass-fronted cabinet sang a ballad to her. It looked like the leaf of a celestial plant.

Celine stuck a wool dress under her chin, its hem like a melted bell. Echo inexplicably knew that the mesmerizing crotchet was done by nimble-handed teenage girls and took a week to get right.

"Look how expensive this looks! It's not like she needs it anymore, and you sure do." Celine kissed the air in front of a fabulous mink coat, then stuffed it into one of the large IKEA bags. "There is just so much stuff here, nobody is even going to notice you took anything."

Echo reached for the shapely peplums and pleats, unable to quite believe she was allowed to touch them. She could feel the spirit of the craftsperson in every sewn trim, every delicate pattern, and felt the rhythm of their movements. She tipped the dead girl's soft leather loafers, one after another, onto her bare feet.

She had no idea how much time had passed when Celine waved her hand in front of her face and said, "We have to go. Make sure you've got everything you wanted."

When Echo cast her eye around the room one last time, there were hundreds, maybe thousands of pieces still left. Celine was right, it looked exactly the same as when they first entered.

"How could anyone who owns a pair of marbled horsehair boots want to die?" She asked aloud.

To leave, they had to walk through the white-tiled kitchen to climb down the fire escape, dragging their bulging bags with them. Echo saw in a tall vase a population of tiny red fish, all of them floating on top like the last pieces of breakfast cereal. There were some potted plants, many of them dead, but which still managed to exude a kind of crinkly prettiness. As she headed straight for the door, Echo noticed a pile of dried-up orange peels with a single cigarette, stubbed on the inside of the orange's hollow skin, floating in the drift across the kitchen counter. Was that the girl's last cigarette?

Once they were outside, Echo looked down at her feet and noticed that she was still wearing the pair of loafers. She had left her old tennis shoes behind.

They walked behind an empty storefront on Rue de Saintonge, where Celine hailed a cab. The driver scooted to a stop just as they reached the corner.

It was difficult to fit all the clothes into the trunk, but Celine packed it down with all her weight. She took out a handbag from the pile and said, "The rest is all yours!"

"Thank you," Echo mouthed to Celine through the window as the taxi pulled away.

"Just call me your fairy godmother!" Celine said, beaming, the light from the traffic flooding her hair from behind.

Later, Echo would think back to this moment and wish Celine hadn't said that. If Celine were her godmother, then this would be a fairy tale. And in fairy tales, sooner or later, the real princesses are separated from the fake ones.

Dust and willow cotton flew past the car window like snow. The driver was playing classical music, a Debussy prelude she didn't know she recognized. A mirror embedded in the mahogany made a frame around her face.

The mirror made her look carefully at the interior of the car. The seats were made of thick, soft leather that warmed her body. When she reached her hand up, she touched the fine-grained suede of the roof. The driver was wearing a crisp navy suit and his superbly articulated hands circled smoothly around the steering wheel, making a blur of his white gloves.

Wasn't the taxi that swerved around the corner for her a Prius?

When she arrived at her apartment, the driver got out of the car and carried her bulging blue bags past the teenagers hanging out in front of the stoop and up the four flights of stairs to her door. He bowed slightly and kissed the back of her hand.

In the next moments, she forgot what his face looked like; when she peered through her window down at the street, the car, and any trace of it, was gone.

. . .

That night, on the slow-crawling Internet that she stole from the Tunisian bistro downstairs, Echo exhumed any information she could find on the previous owner of her new wardrobe, piecing together bits of interviews and blog posts about her life.

Mega Mun was discovered at sixteen trying to sneak into a Parisian nightclub by a well-known photographer who himself was about to quit the business if not for this "creature" who revealed herself to him as a high school student on a foreign excursion. She was a splinter-thin Korean girl who managed to exude the confidence of curves. "Lots of girls try to look small, cross their legs, but Mega makes herself large," the photographer reported to Fashion TV. Mega was known for her fluttering eyelids, which were said to be like French doors shutting against a gale. She was described by numerous sources as indolent, destructive, and sex-crazed.

Although not a single sit-down interview with Mega herself was ever conducted, it seemed many people spoke on her behalf. Narcisco said in an interview, "Mega's crazy, but hipcrazy. Cuckoo! We can relate, you know? She's not boring." She was said to be ignorant of fashion trends, but somehow a mohair jacket or a well-cut trouser morphed her from insufferable child to idiosyncratic aristocrat. A few years ago, it looked as though Mega suddenly dropped off the scene, as if the world that loved her had forgotten all about her.

That is, until she resurfaced on the previous day's fashion blogs. Alone and broke, having spent all her money on clothes, she was last photographed by an amateur street-style photographer walking through the cobblestoned streets of Rue Des Rosiers wearing a @Vetements sweater and *these* @Balenciaga joggers from two seasons ago. A velvet backpack from #Chanel and a pair of platform #Prada loafers with a color between black and brown and carrying a vintage mini Hermès. Then she was seen jumping in front of the train at Métro Pont Marie. She left no note.

Knowing the dates, names, locations, and brands added to Echo's steadily conflicted feelings of having taken all the clothes in the first place. She thought about calling Celine, explaining that she couldn't bear to wear any of it and asking her to put everything back.

But that was just a lie Echo told herself.

The very next morning a woman crossed one of the stone bridges of the Canal Saint-Martin to ask Echo where she'd gotten her jean jacket. Then she was given a free mango lassi at her favorite Indian takeout place. Later that day, while walking to the La Poste, an elderly tourist couple asked if she would accompany them to the opera at the Palais Garnier that night, as they just happened to have one extra ticket. Their daughter had to study that night. Walking across the fountain in the center of the Jardin du Luxembourg, she was photographed in her new Vivienne Westwood gown, and the photo showed up in the style section of *Madame Figaro*.

An anonymous feature on her appeared the following week on *The Cut*. An intern at *Vogue* had created an Instagram account for her and it immediately boasted a million unique daily visits. Stylists called her "Swaggy Librarian meets Ninja Lolita" and "Underground watercolor chic" and other things that made no sense to her. Fashion-school fans swarmed her apartment with their asymmetrical bobs, wanting to know which big-time mogul was funding her, what fashion editor was mentoring her.

"I really don't know what to say," Echo was quoted to have said. "I was just hot, so I took my sweater off, and then my ears were cold, so I put on a hat."

The industry had no choice but to make up a stunt backstory for her: the girl of the moment was named Echo, she was anywhere between seventeen to thirty-seven years old, possibly the heir of a Tencent fortune, or Wanda Group royalty, or the daughter of those people who bought the Waldorf Astoria. It was a decent story, almost as exciting as the ex-con who became a famous model from his mug shot.

Twelve dresses, twenty shirts, three gowns, five coats, and fifteen pairs of shoes had changed everything. Taking the Métro every day to the dingy language school near the Opéra or having a snack in the afternoon in the least popular ramen shop on Rue Sainte-Anne, the only difference for Echo was that she now brought a sensational weekend bag with her so that she could change her outfit and reemerge with a complete and startling transformation. The clothes gave her a cool-eyed confidence; the fabric fibers must have seeped into her skin, into her molecules and bloodstream, changing her very chemistry.

Wearing the dead girl's clothes also gave Echo a new language. This allowed her to transcend social barriers. *Vogue* named her one of the "7 Must-Follow It-Girls of a Quietly Mysterious and Refreshingly Timid Nature." "Echo is bringing orphan lost girl who #speaksbadfrench to the next level," read the caption, which received ten thousand likes and countless emoji hearts. "She always looks delicious, it's like we all want to eat her because she's too tasty!" More likes and cartoon bombs. Tom Ford said he found beauty in her confusion. They all agreed, in Echo, a tremendous fashion star was born.

Important-sounding people told her to *do this, wear this, hold this, stand here, put that heavy triangle on your head* and she did. They told her to *post this, use this, link this,* and then *this,* and she said "Sure." They said *"Très bien fait."* She closed her eyes and they put makeup on her eyelids. *"Bon!"* they said. *"Belle!"* Echo was in demand. She showed up on sets, drank *cafés allongés,* ate *canelés,* earned money for selling clothes, and used that money to buy more clothes. There appeared to be no way of turning off her new powers; it was as if someone had handed Echo a baby. A baby who screamed if she didn't spend every night suited up, turning up at fashion events, drinking cocktails, and saying witty things about seams.

Echo came into moods and desires she was unfamiliar with, and whenever it got too confusing, she just drank more champagne. She began a one-sided affair with a married socialite named Nicholas whose last name was twenty-five letters long. The *Daily Mail* digitally mashed their photos together and labeled them "Smitten." She was pseudo-adopted by his family, who took her skiing in Austria, where she ate delicious cheeses and sat speechless as they sprayed champagne on one another's faces for a week straight.

It was with Nicholas's family on an ambassador's yacht in Crete that Echo got to see a great blue whale. It was fifteen feet long and splashing the water with its tail. The captain beckoned everyone to the deck and Echo watched from the upper deck as the other guests leaned over the side of the boat to pet the smooth skin of the whale's cheeks. Their hands moved right above its mouth. The whale's body was parallel to the boat, and all around them there was sky, then a wall of waves, then sky and more waves.

Clutching her hat to her head, Echo looked deep into the whale's large eye and the whale looked back at her. She thought they reached an understanding. The whale was playing with her, with all of them on the boat. Look, the eye said, I'm just humoring you, you small insignificant being. You? You're not even worth killing.

Despite international efforts, six months passed and the authorities had been unable to locate any part of the missing plane. Beneath the waves in the deepest blue water, whales mistook human signals for the voices of their own kind. The sonar waves emanating from the rescue ships' equipment gave the whales night terrors and anxiety. During these times, they were short with one another. They suffered from their nervousness and it made them miss their mothers. Low-frequency pings gave whales bad directions, to turn left instead of right, up instead of down, and it was only a matter of time before the first whales began washing ashore, dying on the gritty sand beside airport runways.

Six months after inheriting the dresses, gowns, coats, and shoes, Echo's most treasured pieces were beginning to look worn-out or had their zippers broken. Designers gave her more clothes, but there had been no time to wear them and nowhere to store them. She had already gotten rid of all her furniture to make room for shelves for the knits and racks for the dresses. Rows of shoes lined the walls of her room. All of her mementos and family photos, her cheap luggage, her terrible old clothes, had to be put into storage.

Fashion week whirled her across dance floors, cheek to cheek with starlets, and had her running barefoot in the dying grass of the Tuileries. One moment she found herself on the long tables of Dior's dinner in the industrial ballroom of the Palais de Tokyo, pressing a silk pocket square to her small lips. The next she was lined up on Chanel's staircase waiting to have her picture taken. That was when she spotted the first of what she called The Others.

The first one was a tall woman of indeterminate age, whose long hair was so blond it was absolutely white. She stormed through the door draped in a Balenciaga cocktail dress intricately boned at the waist. She grabbed a glass of champagne from a tray and threw it back with an audible gulp. Echo recognized the dress immediately. She squeezed her way down the stairs and put her hand on the woman's shoulder.

Close up, she could see that the cream collar of the dress was stained with lipstick in the front and there was red wine spilled on the hem.

"Excuse me," Echo said. "I love your dress, where did you get it?"

The woman spun around and smiled at her with wine-stained teeth, spilling some of her champagne on the floor.

"Oh, you'd never believe it," she cried. "I got it at the Kilo Shop right on Saint-Germain and it absolutely changed my life. Every time I wear it, I get lucky!" She toppled away, wiggling her hands at the waiter holding the plate of crudités, swaying and spilling, all the while Echo couldn't take her eyes off her.

There were more sightings of women wearing clothes with ironic elegance. Olga from Italy with a gypsy mother who found four pairs of shoes left behind in a hostel bathroom. Finnish Cecil with the shaved head and eyes like precious stones, who spent a semester of tuition money at a consignment shop. A small Japanese woman who stuffed herself into a corset that was too small for her but nevertheless swore that it was made for her.

Afterward, Echo couldn't stop thinking about these mislaid articles drifting aimlessly through Paris and the women who wore them. They were so familiar these women, the delighted awe of new indulgences right there on their faces. Were they all remnants of Mega? Did they recognize it in Echo as well?

On the last night of shows, instead of heading out to the after parties, Echo turned up unannounced at Nicholas's town house wearing a brand-new hot-pink Versace number under her enormous mink coat. But to her surprise, right after taking her coat, he nearly blocked her from continuing on.

"What . . . is going on with your face?" he asked. "Are you sick?"

"What do you mean?" she said, touching her lips and cheekbones with her fingertips.

"Maybe it is this outrageous dress you're wearing. Why don't you go home and change into that slip of yours? You look so nice in it."

"I can't find it." Echo groaned. "I think I left it in that hotel in Tokyo."

"What a mistake," Nicholas said. He shook his head as if he'd never been so dissatisfied with anyone. "You should have never left Asia without it."

Walking home along the left bank of the Seine from his town house, Echo thought she saw another blue whale, spouting water over the river's surface as it swam up alongside the sightseeing ships. Standing there, paralyzed with feeling, she remembered a scene from her childhood—while shopping with her parents, she had cried because she was thirsty. She had hugged their legs and told them she was thirsty, but they were too busy and forgot about her until at last she had burst into tears. They laughed at her then: who cries over being thirsty? But at that moment Echo didn't know how long that terrible thirst would go on for; for all she knew it had been with her forever.

Echo thought of the plane, still missing. The last thing she wanted was for some boat to dredge up a wing, a seat cushion, a waterlogged suitcase filled with cosmetics. Locating the final destination of the missing passengers would mean the end of hope. An enduring mystery was better than just another accidental tragedy. Echo pleaded with the vessels and the radars that they never find what they were looking for.

Had she wanted to, it would have been so easy to walk to her rented apartment, where she would fill her luggage with the dead girl's clothes and then dispose of them in various dumpsters around the city. Her lost-and-found jacket would be waiting for her and she pictured herself pulling it over her bare shoulders with a deep sense of relief. At the edge of the bank, she carefully took one arm out of her long coat and let the other sleeve slide off her arm by the smooth silk lining. The coat landed softly in the murky river and floated away, her trifling gift to the whale. It could hold a lot of secrets, this water. Hers was nothing.

Future Cat

THE WINE AGER had arrived unceremoniously in a big flat box a few days earlier, along with her grocery delivery. Before Maggie read the instructions, she'd completely forgotten what it was and why it had come. It was the color of a brass instrument, the shape and size of an old record, with a groove going through the middle the width of a man's wrist. A shiny button glowed warm and pink from the rim. When pressed, a word popped up in cartoonish letters.

AGE, it read.

Maggie slid a cheap bottle of wine into the groove and pressed the button. Nothing happened. She poured a glass, raised it to her lips, and took a sip. It tasted fine, she thought. Feeling more experimental, she put her basil plant on the plate, pressed the pink button, and watched the leaves shrivel and the stalks go limp. The tiny cactus from the bathroom was more or less unaffected.

At the wine shop downstairs, she picked out a bottle of 2016 Château Margaux cabernet sauvignon that was supposed to improve with time. At home she popped it open, poured two ounces or so into a wineglass, placed the bottle into the groove, and pressed the button. She poured a second glass and then tested them both. It did change the flavor somewhat, the aftertaste of berries lingering in her mouth. The color might have coated her glass longer when she swirled it, but other than that she couldn't really tell the difference.

When the advertisement for this Wine Ager appeared on her computer screen, she couldn't control herself and clicked "buy" right away. She'd recently purged out-of-date iPods, iPads, a VHS rewinder shaped like a Corvette, and a jiggling adhesive mask that was supposed to work out her face. She already had a robot vacuum, a neck massager, an air purifier, a humidifier, and a dehumidifier. What was one more impulsive appliance purchase?

She had been expecting a state-of-the-art high-tech gadget, but the thing in front of her looked more like something someone's mother might pull out of the attic in order to display pomegranates, scented candles, or gourds.

The first living thing Maggie aged to death was a garden snail she peeled off the sidewalk. Her finger hovered over the button before she pressed it. The snail's shell withered away in seconds, turning foul and brown. Then, before she could inspect it, her cat, a black and white rescue named Small Cow, jumped up and knocked the remains under the refrigerator. He tilted his head up at her, eyeing her suspiciously.

"Come here, you," she said while noisily shaking the bag of dried duck organs that gave her magical powers over him. Last summer Maggie had heard Small Cow meowing pitifully in the rain behind a dumpster. She'd brought him home, cleaned the gunk from his eyes, and picked out his fleas by hand in the sink. Still, the callous and unsentimental animal barely acknowledged her without taking bribes. He gently nudged her arm with his head and she rubbed his cute furry face with a pink heart for a nose until a bird flew by. Small Cow went over to the window, got up on his hind legs, and looked outside, like a toddler.

"The box says that it allows you to enjoy young wines without waiting years for them to mature," she told her boyfriend, Greg, over the phone.

"What does?" In the last year Greg had been promoted from product engineer to executive VP in charge of development. Company profits were booming, and the new responsibilities cluttered his brain. "Sorry, what were you talking about again? Wine?"

"My new Wine Ager," Maggie replied. "It just came in the mail today. I have no idea how it works, but it's definitely doing something."

Greg made his usual sound indicating for her to go on.

"Let me read the description to you, okay?" she asked, shifting the phone from one ear to the other so that she could read the box. " 'The Wine Ager™ is made of a patented metal alloy that creates its own electrical field. This field travels continuously between the plate and the individual bottle of wine, interacting with molecules to speed up the chemical reaction of aging. Our special metal alloy acts as a catalyst to drive the aging process without adding any substances to the wine itself while substantially changing its taste and character.' "

She paused. "Are you listening to me?"

"Yeah," said Greg. "Taste. Character. You bought this thing that takes shitty wine, whacks it with electricity, and, boom, it's better tasting. I got it."

"Not necessarily better tasting," said Maggie, "just older tasting. It makes the wine older than, well, I guess it depends on how many times you press the button actually." She put a bag of rock-hard avocados on it. "Actually, it's really sending the wine into the future," she said, then repeated it for emphasis: "The future."

"Anyway . . ." said Greg after a long pause, "what kind of underwear are you wearing?"

She rolled her eyes even though he couldn't see her. Greg's important deadline was to launch a new networking app called Chicken Tinder.

"The big beige ones."

"Why? Just to torment me?" he asked. Being promoted had also made Greg very horny. Maggie guessed it came with the territory of feeling so important so much of the time.

"I'd say they are vaguely medical," she added. "The kind of practical undergarments suitable for someone who is writing something that will probably turn out to be shit."

"You put too much pressure on yourself," Greg said. "What you do is hard. You should go outside, enjoy the nice weather for me."

His tone was so gentle. She wanted to put her eye socket against his shoulder. She didn't know what made her feel worse, when he used to ask about her work or that now he assumed that it was not going anywhere.

Maggie hung up the phone and pressed the button next to the avocados but didn't bother to see what happened to them.

Spring had finally arrived. It was impossible to judge the emotional repercussions of such a long succession of dreary days on Bay Area inhabitants. But it was over. The days were warm enough that her daffodils, no longer frozen, were able to express themselves. At the bakeries down in the Mission, people shamelessly stuffed their faces with fresh strawberry pies. Grown men were taking bites of each other's brownies. Girls stood outside wiggling their winter butts this way and that.

Maggie knew this even though she spent most days inside her apartment, avoiding this mysterious elusive "work" that she called her "book." Ever since she quit her job last fall to focus on it, every attempt at writing made her feel like an imposter. She would rather do anything else. She wanted to eat the pages so they wouldn't exist anymore. Therefore the Wine Ager presented itself as an irresistible distraction. She couldn't seem to leave the damn thing alone. Her brain refused to stop coming up with more things that would benefit from a few extra years to reach peak goodness.

A bottle of soy vinegar went from five years to fifteen in

front of her eyes, and licking a drop off the tip of her finger, she could picture its new journey through ceramic urns in the sun. As she watched the contents go from thin and flat to thick, viscous, and velvety in its bottle, it occurred to her to try it with a sad jar of pickled cabbage. Within seconds, the leaves bubbled with frenzied fermentation, becoming as ripe and pungent as anything her grandmother could have dug out of her cellar.

There were even a few debut novels on her bookshelf she'd put off finishing. With a few rounds on the Wine Ager, she found one novel's narrative tone less grating, as the teenage characters conveyed much-needed self-awareness and wisdom far beyond their years. In another, a central character matured out of the storyline altogether, divorcing her abusive husband and running away to Antigua with a childhood fisherman friend.

Certainly the last thing Maggie wanted was to be two years older than she was, or two months, or two days. She was keenly aware of time lines, expiration dates of food, the shelf life of flowering plants, and the appropriateness of behavior at any given age.

When she first started writing in earnest, she'd been a completely different person. Back in college, she had won writing contests and been bestowed with such titles as "emerging" and "promising."

It was during that boom of minor achievements that she met a chain-smoking dreamboat named Maxi in the student bar where he was playing electric guitar with his hands and a keyboard with his foot. He was an international student from

Moscow with a Cyrillic tattoo across his broad emaciated chest. Plenty of girls already knew what it meant: until we meet again.

Just standing next to Maxi made her feel more like an artist. He struck everyone as a person who can derive all his pleasure from music, as if nothing else, not even what time it was, ever mattered. He taught Maggie how to play the Miles Davis improvisations on the piano, using her stories to write top-line lyrics to melodies. He would pick her up and run around the supermarket with her on his back, singing their song at the top of his lungs. He promised to send the arrangements to the best bands in the country. He made her picture those songs being pop hits in Finland. Jakarta. Japan. When he talked like that, swinging his arms against her cooking pans turned into cymbals, she believed him. Those days they were transcendent, made innocent and immortal with—it seemed so obvious now—all the time they still had in front of them.

She would have been willing to spend the next five years feeling like an artist just standing beside him. She would have followed him from one state to another, hopping from artist residency to colony, drinking cheap Polish vodka, and taking it out on each other in taxis. Because when they talked about the things they loved, it always felt like singing. They made up on people's stoops and kissed in a way that made people call the police. They owned nothing but each other, and that was what they fought over. Who needed to sleep more? Who was busier? Whose career would be more important for the greater world? Which one of them would be the bigger monster?

Then a whole year passed after graduation. Instead of applying for academic fellowships and Ph.D. programs, Maxi convinced her to go with him to an artist residency his poet friend had told him about, on an island without electricity or plumbing that two outdoorsy bros bought off of Craigslist. Huddled together beside a perpetually dying fire, they put lyrics to songs he composed and told each other stories about their families, comparing upbringings in their different communist countries, and that was when Maggie realized how truly impractical both of them were, each in their own way. When she left after three weeks, on a wooden dinghy with a UTI, Maxi chose to stay there alone, happily making analog samples of magpies and birds or whatever.

"Do you have a plan?" she asked him as they said goodbye. "Any plan at all?"

"It's not at the top of my priorities right now," he said. "Whatever is supposed to happen will happen."

She watched him scraping dried mud off his shoe with a stick for a minute before saying, "So you think I'm just going to take care of everything for you?"

"No," he said quickly, not looking up at her. "I wouldn't expect you to do that."

When Maxi's visa expired during his trip home to visit family in Chelyabinsk, he was banned from reentering the country. He asked her to take care when shipping his guitars. Maggie entered an MFA program in the Midwest, but this time she earned very few distinctions. After that, she got realistic about her prospects. She began following a strict set of behaviors, avoiding carbohydrates, dark liquor, and tobacco products. She moved back to San Francisco, where she got a job writing content at a ride-sharing start-up in order to pay off her student loans. The job was boring and made her feel underappreciated, but somehow that gave her a higher opinion of herself, like she had been wronged by a stupid world.

Greg approached her at a networking event. She accidentally slept with him after too many unusually complicated cocktails and then he bought her an iPhone for her birthday. She was charmed by how caring he was toward his younger sisters. Early on during their dating he'd said, "If this doesn't work out, I'll be your older brother," and she surprised them both by bursting into tears. She had to keep going out with him after that so as not to be rude, and before she knew it two years had gone by and he asked her to marry him.

She said she would think about it. Technically, she was still thinking about it.

None of which would explain why, shortly after making herself lunch, she aged her cat. Not a minute after the idea popped up in her head, she found herself hoisting his tubby body onto the dining table.

"Don't move, Small Cow," she said, scooping his tail onto the plate.

Before he could dart away, she pressed the AGE button. Immediately she regretted it. The process itself didn't seem to inflict physical pain, at least not that she could see. Small Cow hacked and coughed a couple of times, but then he stepped off the plate and sat on his haunches, looking dazed.

For the first time he didn't seem all that excited about the duck organs. In fact, he choked on some imaginary mouthful and went to drink from a bowl that wasn't there. Afterward, he misjudged the circumference of the Lucite coffee table, leaned too far forward, and fell off the edge.

The rest of the afternoon Maggie followed him around as he bumped into the carefully curated objects in the living room. She tried to anticipate his movements by repositioning planters and table lamps in his way. The bronze water bowl and food dish were nudged over to new spots beside the ceramic herb planter and to the right of the sofa.

His automatic feeder sounded, but instead of shooting over to scarf down his food in a ghostly blur, Small Cow didn't even seem to notice. It was as if he'd finally gotten over the indignity of his heritage, of having once been a wild thing.

"Greg lets me have a cat even though he's allergic and we had to get a bunch of air purifiers," Maggie remembered bragging to Maxi, the only time she got to see him again. It was he who reached out first. He sent her a message from an unknown number, asking if she was safe. Earthquakes and wildfires, much like terrorist attacks, have the unintended effect of bringing old lovers out of the woodwork. It had been awkward when they met up in front of the restaurant, not knowing where to put their faces when they hugged.

The woman who ended up taking care of Maxi's visa situation was called Samantha, a serene, teenage-looking girl according to the picture he showed Maggie on his cellphone. Maxi tapped his fingers at his screen, talked about Sam, "Sammy," who had grown up on a soybean farm in Virginia but had been working as a concierge at a hotel in Colorado. The hotel was associated with an artist residency and it was while immersed in the scenic mountain splendor of the West that they first met. He inundated Maggie on the details of the elaborate salads Sammy made for lunch and the twins she was growing in her belly. "She's such a sweet person. She's planning on running a kindergarten from our living room," he said, holding up another photo.

"Greg and I could have but we chose not to," Maggie said, her mouth around a chewed-up straw. "You know, if we did, we would have already."

She never told Greg about seeing Maxi again. She kept meaning to bring it up casually, but never did. Now three whole months had passed and it would seem suspect. She did tell her friend Bobbi, during one of their "writing dates" at a Starbucks disguised as a neighborhood bistro. Bobbi had just started an online business and cut her hair into a bob and started applying her makeup cynically.

"Where is this going?" Bobbi interrupted five minutes after Maggie got started. "You didn't, like, have sex with him, did you?"

"What? No. He is married now."

Bobbi stuck her neck out across the table. "So . . ."

"I can't stop thinking about him," said Maggie. "What if he's the love of my life?"

"Maxi? That emaciated homeless-looking guy?" Bobbi laughed. "Greg is a million times better for you. He's so positive and seems genuinely supportive of your work."

"Don't you think he's supportive of my work because he's too dumb to understand that it's garbage?"

"I can't listen to this anymore," Bobbi said, putting up a hand in front of her face and closing her eyes. "This is just a form of procrastination."

"I know, I know," said Maggie, and returned her eyes to her computer. They were sitting there at that unreasonably small table with both their laptops at angles, trying not to spill coffee on their laps. Perhaps this was why most of their friends from college had stopped even pretending to write. They spent their energies pretending to be creative consultants and cultural influencers and other cooler-sounding things. Maxi and Bobbi might have had a fling way back when. Maggie vaguely recalls, or this could be her imagination, once seeing them make out at a party. So it could have been for myriad reasons why Bobbi always asserted that Maxi was nothing special.

Perhaps sensing Maggie's skeptical expression, Bobbi abruptly looked up from her typing and said, "Look, it was a million years ago and you were both idiots. Just let it go."

At around five o'clock that night, Greg asked her to meet him for a quick bite at one of those old-school French restaurants in Pac Heights that was definitely not cool anymore, judging by the color scheme and how courteous the older waiter was when he interrupted them to take their order.

"You feel like eating?" Greg asked, a rhetorical question to which the answer was clearly no.

It was six o'clock. Maggie had two glasses of wine waiting for him and hadn't eaten anything but a fistful of quinoa all day.

No, no. She shook her head agreeably. She wasn't expecting an actual dinner, of course not. No, they'd get a drink before he returned to the office to prepare for an important investor meeting the following morning.

"Sorry, one more email," Greg said, not looking up from his phone as he explained that the cofounders were debating changing directions on the game itself. "They've got this sick interface, but they can't decide if Chicken Tinder is going to be about doing dares or matchmaking for people with chickens."

While Greg typed on his phone, Maggie talked about her adventures with the Wine Ager. She described in detail the pear rotting from the inside out, the wilting of the basil plant, and even the snail, only leaving out the part about her cat living in another dimension.

"So what you're saying is that it's really a time machine," he said.

"Yes!" she cried. "But it's only capable of moving in one direction. Forward."

"That's too bad, huh," he added, one hand on her thigh and the other signing for the check in the air.

"Is that all you're going to say? Don't you want to use it?" she asked.

Greg laughed. He tugged his coat over his shoulders, ready to leave as soon as the check came. "No way. Look at me. I don't have any time as it is!"

If she could make time go backward instead of forward, she would have rewound it to that autumn evening that had felt too short. That night with Maxi, when they talked until the restaurant turned up their lights. Maxi had come close enough to kiss her goodbye, how she marveled and panicked, as if a girl who had been hibernating inside her had just woken up. Even when they were in the deep of it, their skin still touching, her mind had been full of questions, racing ahead. Why had it taken him so long to find her again? And also, where would they live? How could they afford to buy all the crap she was addicted to buying now?

Then it was Maxi who put a stop to it. "Whoa. What are you doing, Mags?"

He was pulling his face away from hers so that a short stack of chins gathered at the top of his neck.

"I can't do this," he said urgently, as if her lips contained a contagious disease. "I haven't even been granted conditional status yet!"

He touched her left earlobe with his thumb and forefinger and she nearly passed out with yearning. "You're funny, Maggie," he said. "I never know what you want from me."

How long had she been sitting there, touching her earlobe, staring vacantly at the old waiter before he asked her politely if she needed anything else. She shook her head. Pretending as if she knew where she was going, Maggie slid off the chair, walked past the other diners, and made a sharp left at the door against the light of the oncoming cars. By the time she turned the corner onto her tree-lined street, she felt absurd and sad.

Maggie stormed up the stairs, slammed her front door, kicked off her shoes in the foyer, and studied her face in the hallway mirror. Her eyes welled up painfully. Maybe it was just a kind of allergy for women of all ages whose bodies could not stand that relentless coming coming coming of spring.

It must have been past midnight, the cafés below her apartment were quiet. Picking up her purse, she walked into the living room where Small Cow seemed to be waiting for her at his perch by the window. Maggie scooped him up as he mashed his smirking face against her arm.

There had been another Small Cow once, a black-and-white fur ball whose name, spoken in the language she grew up speaking, was less cumbersome. She wanted nothing more than to forget that kitten, that language, all those times, but, alas, nostalgia does not care for the suffering it inflicts.

She still remembered the morning at the courthouse when one of Maxi's friends married another person's girlfriend so they could give each other citizenship. Afterward Maggie and Maxi had gone hand in hand to the same immigration lawyer's office. The lawyer leaned in and looked meaningfully at Maggie, explaining the paperwork and interview process, step by step, month by month, year by year, until she could transmit her citizenship to him like a disease.

She shook her head as if to dispel those memories, still pure and aching, and Small Cow scrambled away from her. She didn't have the confidence, the wisdom, to be sure of her decisions. Her past had not yet reconfigured into something she could understand, reordered in a way she could accept.

So there was really no choice. Maggie retrieved the Wine Ager from her collection of useful small appliances in the living room and plugged it in. She tied her hair into a high ponytail and laid her head, left ear down, on the center of the plate. With her eyes closed, she pressed the AGE button. She pressed it again and again. The life of a memory, how long would it take for her to be able to live with it? How much faster could she speed through slow-churning time and grow up?

. . .

Through chambers and tunnels she went, in chilly darkness. A terrible headache lit up her eyes, followed by nausea and her hands going numb. Cold sweats passed through her, but then she relaxed into a meditative state, as if she were watching a fire.

How she would have loved to take the time to taste her next meal with Greg. It would begin with baked eggs in tomato sauce over a slice of five-seed home-baked bread with a sprinkle of sesame seeds, served in a blue dish with white flecks. But then time speeds forward to dinner, and her hair grows a streak of white. Bobbi opens an online store that sells Korean face lotion and becomes a sensational success. Maxi moves to the Pacific Northwest with his wife and children without telling her, and her longing for him falls from her heart like rotten fruit. The dish now is black and the waiter who brings it to Maggie is older than her father, who grows sick and passes away suddenly before her. And at his funeral Maggie notices that beside Greg sits a woman who turns and looks right back into her own eyes. Different possibilities rise to the surface, people revealing themselves to her and then moving to the peripheral darkness.

It was obvious to her that Greg had married her and had done so quickly not just because he liked the way she looked but also because he was really in love with her. He was a big-hearted boy from a broken family. He wanted to provide the gift of a comfortable life, a gift that not many people have to give, and he gave it to her.

As the years moved forward, Maggie's world shifted in an irretrievable way. She was grasping for something in the deep recess of a large cave, traveling through the inner world of her mind, feeling the essence of time and its possibilities. She was awakened to each new truth, which always corresponded to something that she already knew.

How could Maggie possibly have explained it without sounding heartless? Her own parents had spent most of their lives trying to become citizens of this country. She witnessed the years her father wasted working at fast-food restaurants in order to keep earning that useless degree for his student visa. Those months her mother worked as a nanny, nearly for free, for a lawyer's family simply because she needed him to apply for a green card. She knew there was always a price to be paid, higher than anyone ever anticipates. Maggie didn't want to go through any of it again for anyone. Not even for Maxi. She couldn't bear the thought of getting back in that line.

A thousand sunrises and sunsets carry her along the edge of time. As she tumbles further from the age of infinite trajectories, from the outrages of her childhood, from birth. That haunted autumn evening becomes last autumn, the autumn before, and the autumn before that. Stop, Maggie blurts out. Knowing then that she doesn't want to live through the hard moments anymore. She just wants to live! But she is still floating, dazed like a child swept away by a big wave while playing in the surf. Battered from all sides, choking down seawater, arms reaching again and again for the light. She thinks she can hear life calling for her then, like a phone ringing under a pillow. Sooner or later, the present will catch up to her. She will emerge hurled back onto the shore, spitting out sand, crying, shivering and grateful to be alive.

The Art of Straying Off Course

I MET AN architect in my parents' office in Burbank. It was Friday and I was pretending to solve math problems behind my father's desk while the adults gathered around a table covered with blueprints, holding up the scaled model of our future home.

When the architect came to talk to me, he was smiling beneath a full mustache, his green eyes behind strange round glasses. I took his leather jacket and worn tennis shoes as evidence of citizenship in an exciting world. He knelt down so we could talk eye-to-eye and pulled out a briefcase. He extracted from it a light bulb, a golden leaf made of silk, and a rubber doughnut and asked me to pick what I wanted to hold in my hands, which thing I wanted to keep.

Instead, I chose to bring him things. A poem about a watermelon, my grandmother's pearl Mao Zedong button, and a long-stemmed bird-of-paradise. Watching his large hands taking the neck of the flower, I closed my eyes around his smell and learned his name was David.

Years later, he would tell me that he liked me even then, that he had wanted to kiss me right there. Those were the years when I thought he was handsome.

"Forgive me," he said after we slept together in that old hotel in Pasadena.

"What for?" I asked. I had just turned eighteen and I thought I knew everything there was to know about everything. The architect was a concept, a book on the top shelf no young person dared to read. Nobody but me. My hair was everywhere when we kissed. Construction had just been completed on that house but I missed the chance to wake up to that view of the Griffith Observatory. I was going away to college. The architect was too old to be taken seriously. He cupped my cheek with his hand and said, "Go play, explore the world. I can wait for you." I didn't return for seven years.

On the phone, his voice was so far away; we were not experiencing the same rains.

In Cassis I spent all my parents' money on a single silk dress. For a month I couldn't afford to eat anything but baguettes dipped in vinegar. I ran away for days, feeling dark and interesting and free. To my old pal, I wrote a postcard at La Vieille Charité, trying to describe the light in between Corinthian columns.

Someone wrote "I still love you" in Arabic on the walls of

the church's never-ending passageways, but who knew if that was still true.

My mother flew over to meet me in Madrid. She was leaving me, she was leaving my father, and even though our hearts had grown distant, we wept for days over many variations of tapas. "Don't worry about money," she said. "I had the lawyer set up a fund your father can't touch." I do not remember much of anything about Madrid.

After they divorced, they both remarried and individually collected and spawned sets of children I could not keep straight in my head.

During those years I was constantly untangling necklaces and wires.

"You're so lucky. You have everything we didn't have. Now you must go and do something spectacular with your life," my father said, while he rocked one of his new babies to sleep. It was his way of saying goodbye.

I rented an apartment on top of a chocolatier by the Santa Maria La Nova in Naples. Each night the owner offered my friend Rachel and me rum shots in chocolate cups after retelling love stories that I'm sure he made up on the spot. The basement was occupied by a limited bookstore and an out-of-tune guitar. Three women chatted in dialect around a toppling tower of philosophy books.

One night the bartender asked if he could sleep with me, but I was just too tired.

. . .

When in Shanghai all Rachel wanted to do was sleep with cute bar-tenders. "You don't understand. It's not the same thing here." I tried to explain that here the bartenders slept in the booths after the jazz players packed up their instruments and the customers went home. They weren't also trying to be actors.

Only one of them was dumb enough to fall in love with her. He handed over letters, which I roughly translated, and I didn't know whether to laugh or cry. He rowed her around the lake in Century Park in a plastic boat while she texted me gagging noises. I felt so sorry for him. I couldn't really be friends with Rachel anymore after that.

Everything I thought was cool was actually Berlin. Mitte gallery chic, graffiti murals, hookers wearing fanny packs.

I ran into David by accident, in San Francisco outside the SF-MOMA. I thought it was fate.

"I've been traveling, I've seen things!" I told him on an innocent walk across the Golden Gate Bridge.

In Oakland his house was always too cold to stay naked in. David built it himself, so he must have liked it that way. He told me the secret to building things was listening. You had to open yourself to the wants of the materials, the feelings of the stones, the wind and water surrounding the earth, the nature of the wood, and feel their responses to your touch. Then after you reach an understanding, you can play.

I applied for schools, all the while fearful of terrorism both domestic and abroad. I passed exams and qualified for certificates. I tried to keep in touch as best as I could manage. I dyed my hair blue; it turned green and had to be shorn. I decided I was done playing with boys. David was finally forgivably twenty years older than my twenty-six, and I married him.

In Boston there is terrible weather. Girlhood taught me the art of straying off course, but architecture school taught me to stay and make something.

With cardboard and rubber bands I imitated Mies van der Rohe and idolized Frederick Kiesler and De Stijl, the Fascists and Hornbostel. In the studio I built imaginary walls and foundations, then experimented with having no walls and no foundations. I indulged every aesthetic fantasy, strove full-heartedly for fashionable affectations of the time. I toyed with supporting and nonsupporting supports and reached for a building system of tensions in free space. I learned to toil quietly over details no one else could see, to break down the merits of intricacy, to value beauty.

A teenage boy was crying on the train to Philadelphia. I didn't think to help him until I had walked off the platform. My mind was preoccupied with exactness and symmetry. I was rushing toward the taxi stand, armed with prototypes and experiments, off to a conference about glass.

. . .

We fixed up a property on the west side of SoHo next to the Hudson River. "We might never be able to pay your parents back," David said, while measuring the high ceilings of our office. We began our practice in minimalism, using our cunning and being stringent. He built offices and I designed dwellings. He handled big dreams and I found places for childhood toys.

I plotted homes on green vistas with expensive stone facades to highlight panoramas. I wanted to evoke a certain kind of life that would be worthy of future nostalgia. Time passed and people moved through these homes, took photos, and put them on websites.

My ideal clients were nostalgic ambassadors and millionaire wives suffering from a diaspora. I understood them. I gave them my spiel: "We live in a time where we relocate around the globe, native languages are forgotten, and citizenships piled on. Our dwellings must be specially built to re-create that sense of belonging, reinforce the notion of home." For the Japanese ambassador I installed tatami-floor bedrooms in a Midtown high-rise, and a young bride with a thick accent fawned over the Hungarian bath I designed for her Georgian Revival.

I found clever places for HVAC systems, sourced brass doorknobs that looked just like copper, chose and installed the handles on doors I never opened or closed. I looped David in on emails and we made sensible compromises. Clients showed me their Pinterest pages, their Instagram accounts, and said, "Like this and like that, but also like this. Could it be cheaper than this but better?" I carried on the work by devaluing my time.

David and I had a daughter, then another daughter. Decades

ended in cautionary before-and-after tales about aging movie stars with bad plastic surgery.

In Providence, I was asked to teach a course on Le Corbusier's Five Points in architecture school. But instead of supports and roof gardens, I went the romantic route. On the first day of class I asked, "What if life is a space that can be mapped, what would yours look like?" I lectured that the family home was a deposit box of emotions and that reading other people's diaries was just another opportunity to encounter yourself.

During those days, I suffered bouts of panic and bewilderment. I found every explanation troubling. I doubt I was happy, but what good would it have done to know for sure? Peering at me over his glasses at our drafting table, my husband asked, "What now? Really? What do you have to complain about now?"

For long periods of time, people emailed me only if they were promoting themselves. I signed contracts, acquired loans, and paid bills on time. I nursed young children until they were old enough to be sent to boarding school. They returned home changed, fought viciously over their new differences, calling each other terrible names.

I stopped liking his smell and it horrified me. We went on a series of vacations.

In Rome, gypsy children chased us down Via Margutta. They tried to shove their hands into my pockets to get at the few coins inside. David needed my protection then, his bad hip made him lean to the left. Under moonlight in our hotel suite we did not collapse into each other's arms; we streamed shows about the inner lives of serial killers and talked vaguely about beloved dead singers.

We called our daughters sparingly. I could speak well of my children to others, but to them my voice sounded insincere and overblown. I was fearful of such angry, incomplete beings. Should their wanting take the place of mine? Should their accomplishments feel like my own? Must I leave my work to smell their baby heads?

The Amalfi coast is not that far from Naples, but David didn't want to go. "These roads are too dangerous. You should think about my heart condition." He squeezed his eyes shut and grabbed my hand. I could see that the coast was pure fantasy; it was so breathtaking that I was afraid it didn't really exist, that it was just a legend in a cloud. Mermaids must have had homes in the surf and fairies in the hills.

I meticulously documented the modest houses, balconies of flowers, crumbling picture windows that faced the sea.

I knew the hotel project in DUMBO would be our firm's pièce de résistance. I went alone to win the heart of the investor. I promised the hotel would be a work of art, both distinctive and enduring.

"Architecture is not about rationality. It's about irrationality. Everything memorable is irrational," I told him. Holding his eyes, I saw a spoiled childhood become an emotionally deprived adolescence. I saw the philharmonic building in Hamburg with his father's name engraved in stone, where his mother sang, and the hours of waiting that shattered his little boy's heart.

"Let's imagine, in the next biggest superhero movie, where the villain is going to stay?" I leaned close enough to smell his breath. "He's going to stay in your hotel. And nobody, nobody, can ever take that away from you."

We gave a decade over to Brooklyn and the Eleanor Hotel. As it took form, it became known as "awe-inspiring," "important," and "a marquee work of artistry's nuptial with ingenuity," then as the years went on it was deemed the project that finally sank our firm. Construction stumbled upon ancient ruins, which were then accidentally damaged during excavation. Tons of steel had to be brought in. Delays upon delays. Neighbors talked of a curse. Six months before it was due to open, the investor's son threw a party for his friends and one of the fireworks shot into the penthouse and burned the hotel down to the ground.

"Did my face always look gray?" David asked. "Also, where did you put my keys?"

In the morning I made him green juice and at night I checked his heart rate and body temperature. My actions began to feel like an improvised performance I had over-prepared for. "Boys who fell in love with me were never the right ones," I told my youngest daughter. Then because she didn't cry, I said, "You know, I am not your real mother," then, "I'm just joking, I'm joking!"

My parents passed away in quick succession and I did not write down any family recipes. I plucked out my white hairs until suddenly there were just too many. I wore flattering suits until I just wore comfortable pants.

I faulted David for not being young until I became just like him.

Then it stopped being about him at all. It was as if the lights had come on and I was being ushered out of an empty room with brooms. I moved out of the last of the homes I had felt lonely in for so long.

How did I get here? Where is it and when is it that I truly exist? I no longer lived in an age of impressions. Every glance and gesture of people and places can be evoked all at once. I learned to draw on a computer. I sketched ideas by touch, plotted the form on a grid, rendered simple lines into three-dimensional structures, adding details, importing textures, and even inserting people to scale. I could turn any idea into space with complete fluidity on the screen, no matter how big or small or implausible.

Something was beginning to take shape just beyond my reach. The essential part of me that had vanished into architecture. I decided to do the only thing I knew how to do well. I decided to search for proof in the embers. I've achieved beauty and practicality, exactness and symmetry, but what of me is left?

Instead of adding forms where nothing existed, I would recollect the fragments I'd left behind. If I left something in every city I've ever lived, with every person I've ever loved, at every building I've ever called home, then I would go looking.

. . .

Apartment balconies become walk-in freezers in harsh Heilongjiang winters. My family's hibernation supply held an entire side of pig, twenty heads of cabbage, a potato mountain, and a small gathering of persimmons.

A retired mistress of a former client picked me up from the airport in a car that was so crammed with gifts that I had to sit with my feet on a box of single-serving-size milk.

I woke up right as her car pulled up outside my grandmother's block. Relatives were distant and courteous. They stood up straight to hold my hand and didn't ask about my divorce. Most of them had never met me before. In my honor they prepared a braised carp and dumplings, but we ran out of things to say as we ate. I felt an eerie warmth returning, like a concealed joint, once discovered, that would turn the corner to reveal something previously invisible.

"I've seen your picture," my niece's daughter whispered, tugging at my sleeve as I started to leave. "You wrote 'Only for Grandma' on the back."

When we immigrated to California my parents used to count quarters to buy furniture at garage sales but spent dollars per minute on phone calls. The few calls were events in themselves. Mom pressed her mouth to the receiver and I pictured our whole extended family gathered around the phone on the other end. We couldn't bring ourselves to even speak to one another, the only thing phones were good at doing.

"Da Gu! It's Ying," my mother said.

"Oh, sister! How are you? Are you well?" replied my favorite aunt.

"..."

"..." The sound of crying without sound.

Then it was time to hang up.

At first I was disappointed it wouldn't snow in Harbin, but then it started to rain. Here, just as the waters of the Songhua River turned to ice, I awoke again as if for the first time, swaddled in a blanket, on one of the hard seats of a green-skinned train. I remembered opening my eyes to see my mother's face, framed by the sun on the compartment's windows behind her.

My mother did not anticipate my father showing up with me in his arms. The news had not yet begun to report student arrests, and "rumormongering" charges had not yet been dealt. Bullets with eyes had yet to fly, the pipes and bricks did not yet have to go up against the tanks. Each side still thought they would prevail and each side still thought the other outcome would be unimaginable and unacceptable. My mother still had a choice.

The rain carried the scent of jasmine blossoms that led me to the very alley where, on stormy nights, the streets would flood with a foot of water. As a child, I used to float with the neighborhood children in plastic washbasins, splashing and giggling at our marvelous fortunes.

My grandmother would have been watching me when my mother preached about the Hundred Flowers movement, while she learned how to kiss by watching Humphrey Bogart and Ingrid Bergman in *Casablanca*. When she learned how to sing by singing *"L'Internationale."* "Neutrality only aids the oppressor," she would have said. "What do we really have but our moral consciousness?"

It was not difficult to find the very apartment that was my first childhood home, that place between memory and dream. As I approached the door from the commercial street, I saw the sign that advertised it as a "one-hour hotel."

The proprietor with wind-chapped cheeks sat thumbing his phone at the door, and I walked right past him without a word. I thought I felt his eyes on me as I peered out from behind old windows. I ran my fingers along my paint-peeled walls. The balcony contained a display for sex toys. On the walls were numbers for masseuses with glamour shots.

I tried to grasp the particulars of my mother's experience, the foundation upon which she built an unhappy marriage. But I wasn't satisfied with the finish. I couldn't do it without injecting the heroic.

It took first walking out these doors, and then farther still, onto the legal and illegal routes to reach California. My parents waited tables at a restaurant while selling imported kitchen knickknacks out of our one-bedroom apartment, until they bought shiny household appliances to be installed in a suburban house. They earned their citizenship, then spent the rest of their lives importing soup pots, negotiating quotas, sourcing kitchen tiles for discount stores, and becoming rich.

Time slowed, down to the slowest seconds. I stood in the

room of my first steps, my first words, but the distance grew in oblique directions. I sat down on the bed, shrugged off my coat, and watched my right hand holding my left hand, turning around some invisible orb as if to wash it away.

The kite shop had become a restaurant after the park became a road. Before me there was my mother and my mother's mother and hers before that. All these empty rooms filled with their voices, their wants and dreams, their hair falling everywhere.

Strangers who looked like me walked by and threw their ragged shadows against newly erected walls, changing the landscape day after day. Concrete and stone held my remembered paths in place, but with the rise and fall of sun and moon, the beginning moved farther away still. This was all that's left. A gloriously crooked tree once home to birds, named after a river that no longer flowed here. The birds were meant to fly, always and far away.

In the future, my daughters and I will vacation in space. My daughters are elegant as wet swans, so tall they stoop slightly when they bend down to embrace me. Maybe Nadia will be a textile designer by then, Alina a screenwriter, for as long as she can withstand the blows. I avoid their melancholy eyes. I want so much for them both to live carefree lives, but I tell them everything. Maybe everything is too much.

It is a long drive to the hotel, the one on the very edge of the earth. The last stop to rest before we go interstellar, the last place we have never been. In the car, we wrap ourselves in woolen blankets to keep warm. I reach over and stroke Nadia's cheek. I look at Alina, asleep in the backseat, her hands clasped like a schoolgirl's.

"Are you leaving or returning?" asks the young attendant behind glass. I point with one finger to the direction ahead and he waves us through.

The road leads us to a brutal glass-fronted facade, steel balconies cantilevering through the clouds. There are no shadows in space, only the most perfect lines. Travertine steps the height of sycamores unveil marble arches and colonnades. The columns surround a formal pool to reflect the dome. It is then that I feel the recognition run through my body—I've seen this place before. The hotel and the shuttle to space, have I been there, too?

Behind me, through the window, all the places I am trying to leave behind. All that wonderful chaos, horizontal, never-ending.

ACKNOWLEDGMENTS

For this book to make it to the world, I owe an enormous debt of gratitude to the patience and care of so many mentors, institutions, colleagues, and friends.

To Parisa Ebrahimi, my cherished editor and a true kindred spirit. It is such a privilege to work with you. Thank you for loving my book and for the care you took in making it better. To all the wonderful people at Hogarth who work behind the scenes and between the lines, thank you for having faith in my stories.

To my fearless agent Claudia Ballard, who opened so many doors for me. You are simply wonderful.

To University of Southern California, especially Aimee Bender, T.C. Boyle, and Carol Muske Dukes for the early encouragement. To Columbia University School of the Arts, especially Ben Marcus, Donald Antrim, Gary Shteyngart, Victor LaValle, and Binnie Kirshenbaum for an extraordinary education.

To the Wallace Stegner Fellowship at Stanford University, for giving me the tremendous honor that still humbles me to this day. To Elizabeth Tallent, Tobias Wolff, Eavan Boland, and Adam Johnson for courage and inspiration. To all the talented writers in my cohort: David Hoon Kim, Anthony Marra, Shannon Pufahl, Helen Hooper, Joshua Foster, Dana Kletter, Justin Perry, Nina Schloesser, NoViolet Bulawayo, Nicole Cullen, Monique Wentzel, Austin Smith, Lydia Fitzpatrick, and Justin Torres. I don't know how I got to be so lucky.

To the MacDowell Colony, the Corporation of Yaddo, the New York Foundation for the Arts, the Lower Manhattan Cultural Council, the Elizabeth George Foundation, the Cité des Arts, the Bread Loaf Writer's Conference, the Napa Valley Writers Conference, and the Jerome Foundation, I am forever grateful for your life-changing gifts of time and space.

I need to thank and then apologize to my brilliant friends whom I subjected to reading countless drafts of these stories, Wistar Watts Murray and Elysha Chang. And to Orion Jenkins who read every draft twice. Your gentle and thoughtful attentions helped me send them off.

To friends who read and listened, to friends who printed my pages on their office printers, fed me, reassured me that I was a real person, and were so nice to me when I did so little to deserve it: Mike Fu, Charlotte Cho, Jackie Kan, Helen Mun, Bao-Viet Nguyen, Diane Chang, Diana Lin, Christine Chen, Hilary Leichter, Diana Khoi Nguyen, Paul Legault, John McManus, Diane Cook, Elizabeth Reinhardt, Taeyoon

Choi, Derek Yang, Hanna Pylvainen, Maxim Duncan, and Liana Finck.

To Lauren Groff, Emily Graff, Alexandra Kleeman, Yan Sze Li, Seth Fishman, and Denise Shannon whose generous advice came at all the crucial moments.

To Beijing, for the days of my youth, and for giving me back my mother tongue. Thank you for the memories and the lifelong friends.

To my family: Mom, Dad, Uncle, and grandparents, for the unconditional love. Thank you for teaching me to value kindness and generosity above all else and for encouraging me to try my hand at being an artist. To the ancestors, the well from which I drink, for all the rest.

To Paul Chan, who brought so much beauty in my life, and even more laughs. Thank you for always believing in me.

ABOUT THE AUTHOR

XUAN JULIANA WANG was born in Heilongjiang, China, and moved to Los Angeles when she was seven years old. She was a Wallace Stegner Fellow at Stanford University and received her MFA from Columbia University. Her work has appeared in *The Atlantic, Ploughshares, The Best American Nonrequired Reading,* and the Pushcart Prize anthology. She lives in California.